'Who is it?' she said. 'What do you want?' She did not feel frightened and wondered how she could feel so self-possessed when a moment ago she had recoiled from fear at a bat.

'Who's there?' she asked and thought she heard a murmur, a voice trying to break through a barrier between them, a voice distant yet near.

He wants to tell me something, but I cannot hear him, she told herself, and was impatient at her helplessness to understand.

She knew it was the boy she had drawn. He was trying to reach out to her and she stretched out her hand, wanting to grasp him, but instead she found only the clinging threads of a cobweb and drew her hand back in distaste.

Something swooped near and again unreasoning fear of the bats took hold and she decided daylight was better for exploring.

She retreated to the door, but the echo of a voice seemed to call to her to plead to her to stay. 'Listen,' it seemed to say. 'Listen.'

The Council's plan to build over Adam's Common horrifies Peggy Donovan. The wild, unspoilt piece of land is all that makes Peggy's life bearable in grimy Traverton. But more than that, a strange sense of mystery draws her to the common and to its ruined old house. When Peggy glimpses the shadowy figure of a boy who seems to want to talk to her, she knows that the fate of Adam's Common lies in answers hidden in the past.

D1328761

ADAM'S COMMON

DAVID WISEMAN

Queen Anne High School Support Centre

CORGI BOOKS

ADAM'S COMMON
A CORGI BOOK 0 552 52511 1

First published in the USA by Houghton Mifflin Company 1984
First published in Great Britain by Blackie and Son Ltd 1987

PRINTING HISTORY
Corgi edition published 1989
Corgi edition reprinted 1989

This book is set in 11/12 pt Century Textbook
by Colset Private Limited, Singapore.

Corgi Books are published by Transworld Publishers
Ltd., 61–63 Uxbridge Road, Ealing, London W5 5SA, in
Australia by Transworld Publishers (Australia) Pty. Ltd.,
15–23 Helles Avenue, Moorebank, NSW 2170, and in New
Zealand by Transworld Publishers (N.Z.) Ltd., Cnr. Moselle
and Waipareira Avenues, Henderson, Auckland.

Printed and bound in Great Britain by
Cox & Wyman Ltd., Reading, Berks.

For Francis

ONE

Peggy Donovan got her things ready for school unwillingly. She had been excited at first when her father told her of his new post in England. She had heard so much about England – its gardens and castles, its quaint ceremonies, its pretty thatched cottages – and she had read so much of its history.

But Traverton was not her idea of England, not at all. It was a grimy industrial town, with narrow, litter-cluttered streets, grey modern buildings, shoddy shop fronts – or, at least, what she had seen of it was. She hated it.

She tolerated school. She had only had two days there so far, but what she had seen was not much to her liking. The school was in the centre of the town and seemed itself to be part of history, but not the romantic history she was familiar with. It was a gaunt edifice of red and yellow brick, with not a tree or blade of grass in sight; although inside, she had to admit, someone had tried to brighten it up with potted plants.

She put on her school uniform. This, she thought, is the worst part of all. It was made of a drab brown serviceable material, and she felt its cut made her look even gawkier than she was. Everything about it, from the regulation brown brogues to the dull tie at her neck, was designed to offend.

'I wish I didn't have to wear this,' she complained to her mother.

'You wouldn't want to be different from the others, would you?' came the reply.

'I wish I wasn't so tall,' she said.

'It's no use wishing. You'll have to make the best of it,' said Mrs Donovan, smoothing Peggy's long fair hair. 'Besides, I've never found it a disadvantage.'

No, thought Peggy, looking admiringly at her mother's statuesque figure, but you don't have to go to school anymore.

'That will be Steven,' said her mother, when a knock came at the front door. 'I hope he's looking after you.'

'Yes, Mum,' said Peggy. Steven Walsh, the boy from next door, had been asked to show her the way to school on her first day and they had quickly become firm friends. He was her only friend so far, for none of the girls at school had shown anything but curiosity about her. Sometimes even Steven could be annoying, as at their first meeting when he had said, 'Are all American girls as tall as you?'

'What's wrong with that?' Peggy had said, her temper ready to flare.

'Nothing,' he had answered hurriedly. 'I like tall girls anyway.'

She thought he was joking, but she was pleased all the same.

'Hi!' he said now, waiting on the doorstep while Mrs Donovan gave her daughter a final, critical inspection.

They walked along the road together and

entered the common, Adam's Common, the locals called it. This was the only feature of life at Traverton that Peggy liked. In fact, she admitted to herself (but to no one else), it was more beautiful than Boston Common and the Public Garden together, wilder, more unspoiled. She felt it was disloyal of her to think this, since Boston was her home. Boston, Massachusetts. She sighed. How she missed her friends there, and lively down-town Boston, and those weekends at Cape Cod.

'Get a move on,' called Steven, racing ahead of her across the common.

She could not hurry across Adam's Common. The green wilderness of Adam's Common stretched a long arm into the centre of the town. To cross it to school gave a glorious beginning to the day. On her first walk there she had seen a flight of greenfinches. It had seemed magical to her, and from that moment, though she hated everything else about Traverton, she was recon-ciled to it through her love of the common.

Steven was waiting for her at its edge, where the green changed to concrete, where the busy Parade bordered it. The Parade was noisy, with people selfishly thrusting their way to work, and reeked with the fumes of trucks, cars, and buses impatiently crowding the streets. How horrid it was, she thought, and looked longingly back to the trees and grass and hedgerows.

She accepted school in spite of the uniform and her feeling of strangeness. In time, she supposed, she would be accepted as one of them, but so far she felt she did not belong. Apart from Steven, the boys were brash and forward. She thought the girls might be ready to make friends, but no one had made a move yet. The teachers treated her as if she were some creature from outer space. She expected they would grow out of it, or she would become used to it.

'Social studies this afternoon,' said Steven, 'with Dicky Richards. You'll like him, but watch out for his ear.'

'What's wrong with his ear?'

'Keep your eyes on him. Whenever he gets riled, he starts to pluck at his ear. The left one. You have a look. You'll see it's a good inch longer than the other one.'

'Don't be silly.'

'It's true, you'll see. You've been warned. Watch out for trouble if he starts. Tom Brookes is the one who gets him going.'

Peggy did not believe him, but that afternoon, when she went into the social studies lesson and was introduced by Steven to Mr Richards as 'the new girl from Boston – in America, sir,' she observed him carefully. It was true; his left ear was longer than his right, and it looked red, as if this last class had been very irritating.

'Yes, Miss Donovan?' said Mr Richards, provoked by her careful study of him.

Peggy blushed and went to the desk he indicated. 'And Walsh,' Mr Richards said, 'I think we'll separate you and Brookes.'

Peggy saw Steven had slipped to the back of the room to sit next to Tom Brookes.

'Oh no, sir,' protested Steven mildly.

'Oh yes, sir,' said Mr Richards. 'Here, next to our American friend.'

Why can't they forget that and just treat me as one of them? thought Peggy. She knew the teacher meant to be kind, but she hated having attention drawn to her. She was sure it would

10

make the other girls resent her. Her mind drifted to thoughts of home, to the friends she had left behind. She wished . . .

She realized Mr Richards was speaking for her benefit, about something called the Trafford Award.

'We've been working hard this term,' he was saying. 'At least, some of us have,' he added, with a significant glance at the group of boys near Tom Brookes. He turned to Peggy. 'It's been in connection with the Trafford Award. That's a prize for the pupil or group of pupils in the town who have made the best contribution during the year to the well-being of the community. Town School hasn't been near winning it for years. Valley School has outshone us.'

A groan rose from the boys at the back.

'The Valley School,' repeated Mr Richards. 'Last year they produced a very fine pageant of the town's history. You remember, Brookes? It was very impressive.'

'It was all right, sir,' Brookes conceded reluctantly.

'This year,' said Mr Richards directly to Peggy, 'we're determined to be the winners. We've been working on a survey of the town's amenities, to try to find out the sort of thing the citizens want – swimming pools, libraries, children's playgrounds, shopping areas, and so on – and compare them with what there is.'

That won't take long, thought Peggy, but was wise enough to keep her thoughts to herself.

'You've joined us too late to be able to take much part,' said Mr Richards. 'But you'll find it interesting. We've divided ourselves into teams for the purpose of the survey. I think we'll attach

11

you to Marion Harper's team. Marion.'

'Oh but sir,' protested the girl referred to, a pretty girl who managed to make even her school uniform look stylish, 'she doesn't know anything about the town.'

'Then,' said Mr Richards, not at all influenced, 'you'll have to tell her all you know. And you'll find a fresh mind useful.'

Marion turned to look hard at Peggy. She doesn't want me in her group, thought Peggy. I wonder why. It had something to do with Steven, she thought. But she could not help it if Steven preferred her company to Marion's.

'Sir,' came the voice of Tom Brookes from the rear of the class.

Mr Richards looked in Tom's direction. Peggy saw his hand move slowly to his left ear.

'Sir,' repeated Brookes.

'Get on with it then,' said Mr Richards, gently stroking his ear lobe.

'Please sir, I thought you'd like to know, because it makes a difference to our survey,' said Brookes.

'What does?' The movement of the hand on the ear was still slow and gentle, Peggy saw.

'The news about Adam's Common,' said Brookes hurriedly.

'What news, Brookes? Get to the point, boy. Tell us what you know, if it's worth telling.' He gave a sudden sharp tug at his ear. The rest of the class was silent, but not Brookes.

'S-sir,' he stuttered, in getting his news out quickly. 'They're going to build on it, sir, a new shopping mall, and offices at the town end, and houses farther on, and an industrial estate at the lower end.'

12

'They're going to do what?' Mr Richards sounded incredulous. His hand had fallen from his ear and he was looking intently at Brookes.

'How do you know this? There's been nothing in the papers.'

'My father, sir. He's chairman of the Planning Committee.'

'Should you be telling us this, Brookes?'

'I don't know, sir,' said Brookes unhappily. 'I just thought you ought to know.'

'Thank you, Brookes. It's very noble of you.' Mr Richards spoke without sarcasm. 'We're very grateful for the information.'

Peggy had listened to the exchange between the teacher and the boy without interest at first, but then she understood what had been said. Adam's Common, the only thing that made living here bearable, was to be covered with bricks, long lines of streets, office blocks, and factories; the trees would go, the grass would wither, the wilderness would be tamed, and instead of her day beginning with the fresh air and birdsong of the walk across the common, it would start with blaring horns and traffic smells. The pond, with its reedy island, the home for breeding ducks, would be covered, to make way for multistoried car parks and more supermarkets.

She realized Mr Richards was looking at her. She must have given voice to her horror.

'They can't do it, can they?' she said in appeal.

Mr Richards was silent for a moment.

'We shall have to wait and see, shan't we?'

TWO

As she walked home with Steven that afternoon, across Adam's Common, she became, with each step, more and more upset at the thought of the changes planned. She did not know how soon the work was due to start, but she feared that, at any turn, she might meet building workers and their equipment. But there was no sign yet of any such invasion, and she began to wonder if Tom Brookes had been scaremongering, making a wild rumour out of a chance remark of his father's.

'Why is it called Adam's Common?' she asked Steven when they stopped at his house. He couldn't tell her, and his mother, when they asked her, did not know either.

'But we've called it that ever since I can remember. I expect your Mr Richards at school will know.'

Peggy shook her head. She had asked him. He had said he had tried to find out from the town records, but most of them had been destroyed during the war when a stray bomb had landed on the building where the archives were stored.

'It won't be Adam's Common much longer,' Steven said.

His mother looked at him in surprise. 'Have you heard already?' she said. 'I thought it was a secret. Mrs Brookes told me to say nothing. She was quite excited, though I must say I don't like the idea. When I was a child, I wandered all over the common, and I've loved it ever since. It's a magical place. Perhaps you find that difficult to understand, Peggy.'

It's not difficult, said Peggy to herself. I feel the same. It has cast its spell over me.

'It's a lovely place,' she said aloud. 'I can't think why they want to spoil it.'

'Money, I expect,' said Mrs Walsh.

Peggy did not mention the news about the common to her mother and father. She did not think they would be interested, for they were too busy settling into their new life in Traverton, where Peggy's father's Boston firm was planning to establish a branch factory.

Peggy's mother, however, noticed her daughter's unhappiness.

'You'll soon settle down and make friends,' she assured her.

I hope so, thought Peggy, but Steven is the only real friend I have. Everything else about the place is hateful, she said to herself when she went to her room. But then she looked out of her window to where she could see the tips of the oaks that bordered the common. I hate it all, all except Adam's Common, and that's going to go. How can they do such a thing?

When she woke the next day, Saturday, she went to her bedroom window again to look out. The trees of the common beckoned to her. She would go and explore the common properly, get to know its every corner, become familiar with every turn and path, store every detail in her memory against the time when it would no longer be there.

She picked up her knapsack with her sketch-pad and some sticks of charcoal, almost without thinking, and left the house. She had always taken her drawing materials with her when going for a walk at home. Perhaps it was a good sign that she was doing the same now.

She crossed the road and entered the common. Previously she had only followed the paths that led across to the town. Now she turned left and away from the town where the common, stretching into the distance, seemed even wilder, unplanned, free. It was a huge open space, rich with green, ignoring the twentieth century, keeping at bay the advance of concrete.

Just beyond the shelter of the oaks on the common's edge was a long wide stretch of grass, rolling in gentle slopes and dips to the distant woodland. Here a group of boys were kicking a football about. They had put their jackets down as makeshift goals. She saw Steven Walsh among them and stopped to watch for a moment.

He was clever with the ball, controlling it as it came to him, then, with nimble feet and a jigging run, evading first one and then two boys who tried to rob him of the ball. He came near Peggy without seeing her and in a moment of daring she ran at him, and before he was aware, had dispossessed him and taken the ball toward the goal. The other boys stared at her, either in surprise or annoyance, she was not sure. Out of the corner of her eye she saw Steven coming to tackle her; she side-stepped and nonchalantly kicked the ball through the goal.

16

'Hey!' yelled one of the boys. (Tom Brookes, she recognized.) 'Who asked you to join in?'

Peggy shrugged her shoulders, pouted, and walked away. Steven called after her. 'You can kick around with us, if you want.'

She was tempted to stay but turned and waved. 'I'm going for a walk,' she called. And, as she went on, she was glad of her decision, for she was discovering more of Adam's Common with every step.

Past the rolling grassland there was a wider area of woodland; paths wound among the trees without any sense of direction, aimless and haphazard. Here there was no sound of town traffic, only the twittering of small birds as they flew in and out of the bushes. It was time for nest building, Peggy thought, as a blackbird scuttered past with a straw in its mouth. She heard a drumbeat and recognized the sound of a woodpecker. She strolled along, content to absorb the delights of nature, but hoping she might come upon a part of the common where she could sit and sketch.

She came to a point where several paths met in a clearing, each leading in a different direction. She stood for a moment as if considering which she should follow, but in truth she had no doubt. One path drew her; in a subtle way it was different from the others, less used, somehow secret. Dense undergrowth encroached upon it; the trees above hung closely down. As she put her foot to the track, she knew it would lead somewhere interesting.

A nearby movement startled her and she turned to see a squirrel vanishing round the trunk of a tree. She penetrated farther along the path, brushing aside the brambles and briars that folded in about her. She refused to be discouraged. She had wanted to follow this path and she would follow it, wherever it led. Along it she would find what she was looking for.

What was she looking for? A place to sketch, she told herself, that was all, something to capture the spirit of the common, something to remember it by.

She swung the knapsack over her shoulder and walked on. The dappled green of the leaves threw glancing patterns across the path as the sun rose higher and struck warmly through the trees. She wished now she had put on a summer dress, it was so close; her old jeans and sweater were uncomfortably hot. Next time she came she would wear something cooler.

The path narrowed and the undergrowth grew more dense so that the green seemed to press upon her. It was still and private here, and, though she felt a small tremor of unease at the silence that surrounded her, she knew this was her kind of place. It was secret, unwilling to reveal itself to just anyone, but, if she was careful to respect it, she felt it would allow her to get to know it.

The path had become so narrow that it had almost disappeared, and she saw that, a few yards ahead, it did in fact come to an end in a man-made barrier of barbed wire, linked through branches cut from nearby bushes. And nailed to one of the branches was a notice, faded with age but legible and precise still: NO ENTRY – STRICTLY PRIVATE.

Peggy Donovan was not known for her patience, and now faced with this sudden obstruction, she was cross; she became more and more angry as she looked at the notice. She had come along here with the intention of finding whatever lay at the end of the path, and no warning notice was going to stop her. Whatever the consequences, she had to go on. She did not pause for wiser, second thoughts to influence her; she peered through the branches, past the wire, and saw that, beyond the barrier, the path opened up again, leading ... where? She had to know. She turned aside from the barrier, and without thoughts to the thorns grasping at her, she forced her way through the undergrowth until she had by-passed the obstruction and reached the path beyond.

'There!' she said aloud as if to let whoever had put up the notice know of her defiance. 'There!' And with a new swing to her shoulders, she set off again along the path.

Then she saw it – what she had come to find! In the distance, standing beyond a field of uncut grass and thriving thistles, was a house, or what remained of a house. As Peggy came out of the trees and saw it, she stopped. It was a picture waiting to be drawn. She only hoped she would be able to do it justice.

The sky was blue, with a few high, almost motionless white clouds; the grass was all shades of green, and dotted with purple and yellow from the wild plants; there was a single tree, dark and distorted as if struck by lightning some time past. And the house! It was built of brick and stone, and its roof, where still remaining, was made of red tiles. The sun, catching the walls and roof made the colours vivid and striking. Peggy could not have imagined anything more perfect for her study. She was sorry she had only brought charcoal with her, and not her pastels. This was made for colour.

But charcoal would have to do, and with it she would be able to catch the light and shade, the atmosphere, the interesting shapes of the ruins.

As she studied it from afar, she thought she caught sight of a movement near the house, as if a door had opened. Surely no one could be living in such a place.

She hesitated a moment, remembering the notice, NO ENTRY – STRICTLY PRIVATE, which she had ignored. Perhaps she ought to turn back; but that thought did not stay with her long. She was captivated by the house and must go nearer to it and sit to sketch it.

She walked toward it, through the long grass, pushing aside the immense thistles that had taken hold. She thought again that she saw a movement at the front of the house, but whatever it was, it was too quick or too furtive for her to tell what had caused it.

The field came to an end at a ditch that separated it from what must have been the garden to the house. There was what might once have been a rockery, with low-growing plants clinging to the stones. She found one rock that was larger than the others and warm from the sun, and sat upon it and took out her sketchpad. She studied the house through half-closed eyes.

Then she opened her eyes wide, for again she had the feeling that something had moved, in and out of the door of the house. She had the feeling she was being watched by someone, or something. She did not move from the rock but sat, quiet, unstirring, not wanting to draw attention to herself.

After a few moments of sitting still, she decided she must have imagined the movement. Or perhaps some wild creature, a mouse maybe, had caused a rustle in the grass.

She returned to her study of the house. When she had first seen it from the edge of the woodland, it had not looked very big, but now she saw it was quite large – or had been, when it was whole. For it was no longer complete. It was a two-storey building, with a wing jutting out at either end. The left wing had been destroyed by fire. Tiles from the roof were missing and timbers could be seen, great blackened beams. The windows of the house were square, deeply set into the walls, with stone mullions. There was a thick climbing vine clutching to the walls and windows. The vine, and the peeping windows, and the charred oak beams, all made the house more picturesque, and commanded Peggy to attempt to draw it. If only she could! If only she could capture the magic and mystery of the place! For, as she studied it the more, it was its mystery that moved her.

She took her charcoal stick and began to block in the shape of the house against the sky. It defied her skill. Try as she would, she found it impossible to capture the ruined outlines. She looked for the box in which she kept her eraser and was annoyed to find she had forgotten it. Impulsively, she tore the sheet from her sketchbook and threw it to the ground. A sudden breeze caught it and carried it away to the door of the house. She got up to go after it but decided she would collect it when she had finished.

She sat down and tried again. This time she started with the other wing of the house, the one that showed less damage. Here too the vines grew thickly, creeping up the walls, around the windows, and reaching to the lead pipes and gutters.

She was more successful this time, at the start at any rate. But when she came to the ruined wing, she again found herself unable to get the shape right, the jutting timbers and jagged ends of brick would not be put on paper, not today, she decided. She would come back some other time and try again. She realized anyway that time had passed and her mother would be expecting her back for lunch. She put pad and charcoal into her knapsack and set off for home. She had taken only a few steps when she remembered the sheet of paper lying at the door of the house. She must not leave it there. She had an aversion to litter and was always careful to clear up after sketching outdoors.

She turned back to the house and was again aware of movement and was certain that someone was watching her from within the house. She had no right to be here but, she told herself, she was doing no harm, so no one could object. Still, she felt that whoever it was inside was observing her every move. She would pick up the page from her sketchbook and leave.

She reached the door. It was closed, though earlier it had seemed to her to be open. She could not see her sketch. There were leaves brought here by the wind, brown and dead, from last autumn, but there was no paper. She was certain it had blown here. She had seen it, lying at the door. But it was not there now.

She heard a rustle behind her and turned rapidly. A ginger cat was peering at her from an untidy clump of growth. It leaped into the grass and was lost to sight. That's what the movement was, Peggy told herself, glad there was an ordinary common-sense explanation for her feelings. She forgot her search for the missing sketch and turned for home.

THREE

William Trafford sat at the window of the library in the west wing of Trafford Court, looking out to the garden and beyond, to the meadow and woodlands; he was dejected and lonely, resentful that he was confined to the house.

It was nonsense, he thought. The cholera that was ravaging the town, in this year 1849, could not reach to his comfortable home. He did not know why his parents could not understand: he was healthy, disease could not strike at him.

He supposed his parents were wise to be careful, but he saw no reason, if his father went into town regularly to meet the new railway engineers, why he could not go with him. If it was safe for his father, why not for him?

He heard his father moving on the stairs, calling to a servant to summon Bradley the coachman.

William left the window seat and went into the hall. His father, being helped into his dark overcoat by his wife, did not notice William. He took his shiny silk hat, put it jauntily on his head, and turned to his wife.

'There! Satisfied?' William watched as his mother straightened the cravat at his father's neck.

'Handsome enough for you?' William's father stepped back to be admired.

'Be careful, my dear,' said his wife. 'You're not going to Riverbank, I trust?'

'Don't worry your pretty little head. My meeting with the engineers is higher up, where the railway is to cross the river. The new viaduct. It's a lovely thing, or will be when it's finished.' He turned to see that William was looking eagerly at him.

'Well, William? Come to see me off?'

'Can I come with you? To see the new railway?'

'Well . . .' His father sounded uncertain.

'No,' interrupted William's mother. 'He can't. He must stay here in the house, until the cholera's abated.'

'Mother!' protested William.

'No,' she said firmly. 'We don't want you mixing with the town children, nor going into town. The air's bad there – poisonous even. I don't like you out of my sight at a time like this.'

William looked to his father for support.

Mr Trafford shook his head. 'Better do as your mother says, William. It's fearful the way the disease has taken hold in some parts of the town. There are tens of deaths every day down at Riverbank and Angel's Meadow. The gravediggers can't cope, and they say it's worse in London and the other big cities, worse even than it was in the last outbreak, seventeen years ago, in eighteen thirty-two. Do as your mother says, William. Keep safe indoors, away from danger. The railway will still be there when all this is over. You'll see. The railway will last longer than the cholera.'

'I want to see it being built,' said William stubbornly.

'There's noise and muck and men,' said his father, taking hold of William's shoulder. 'You'd not find that so exciting.'

I would, said William to himself. I would meet the engineers, and that's what I want to be one day, an engineer, a bridge builder, a designer of locomotives.

'Dreaming again, I see,' said his father smiling down at him.

William put his hand on his father's arm. 'Please, Papa. Let me come with you. Please,' he said urgently.

His father frowned with displeasure.

'We have said no, your mother and I. That's all that needs to be said.'

William turned away and went back to his window seat in the library, angry at his parents. He did not move from the window when his mother came into the room. He knew she was standing at the door watching him, waiting for him to turn, but he kept his back obstinately toward her.

'You're very precious to us, William. You're all we've got. Please understand. We cannot risk losing you too.'

William did understand. His two younger brothers had died three years ago of smallpox. He remembered the distress of that time. He hated to be reminded of it.

'I know,' he said gruffly, but still did not turn to look at his mother. He knew if he did that she would give way to tears, and he hated that.

He heard his mother leave the room and close the door on him. She would be going to the back of the house to the domestic quarters. For a moment he thought of slipping out of the library and through the side door into the garden. From there it was only a mile or two to the new railway construction. He could be there and back in an hour, see where the viaduct was, and return before anyone missed him.

William resisted the impulse. He knew his mother's anxiety and did not wish to hurt her, even though he resented the curbs on his freedom.

He would have to satisfy himself by examining the plans and drawings that his father kept in the library. He opened a drawer in the large plan chest by the fireplace and took out a roll of paper. He unfastened the tape that bound it, spread it on the floor, and, with a book at each corner to keep it flat, he studied the plan. An elaborately lettered title showed TRAVERTON TO THORNSIDE LINE. He could follow the line of railway as it was planned, to cross the river by the new viaduct, and striking through the heart of Riverbank, the cholera-ridden district his mother feared so. He idly wondered what would happen to the people living there, but the railway was not to be denied, he knew.

With his finger, he followed the dotted line marked across the map. He wished he could be there to see the men at work, to watch as they conquered the obstacles in their path. 'Noise and muck and men,' his father had said, not seeing how exciting that was. This was the railway, the iron road, that was going to change the destiny of Traverton. The railway was going to bring a new prosperity to Traverton and the region around. He had heard his father argue this with other landowners. Most of them opposed the railroad, but his father had ignored them and, by permitting passage of the line over his own land, had eased the problems of the railway engineers.

William knew from his father that now there were problems of a different kind. The building of the viaduct was proving awkward, but the engineers would overcome any difficulty. William knew that Joseph Locke, the man in charge, had been a pupil of the great George Stephenson himself. He would not admit defeat.

William sighed. He wanted to meet Mr Locke. I shall be a great engineer myself one day, he told himself, as he rolled up the plan and returned it to the drawer. He went back to the window and dreamily imagined himself standing on a hillside, gesturing to his workmen, guiding them to follow the right line across country. His name would one day rank with the great ones – George Stephenson, Joseph Locke, Isambard Brunel, and he added, William Shelton Trafford.

He sighed again. How could his father, who knew and approved his hopes, deny him the opportunity to watch the engineers at work?

William plucked at the curtain. He looked out at the rockery with its closely planted growth. It was neat and well tended. It was his mother's delight, for she had built most of it herself, once the stones had been brought from the Trafford quarry on the other side of the river. The rockery ended with a dip in the ground – a ha-ha it was called – that separated it from the meadow beyond. Sometimes there were cattle grazing in the meadow, but not today. The farm workers must have moved the herd to the south fields.

Beyond the meadow the woodlands began, and beyond the wood was grassland and parkland that led almost to the centre of the town. It was all Trafford land and would, he supposed, one day be his. He liked wandering through the woods, when he was allowed to. He could see no reason why he was forbidden to walk there now, for the estate was bounded by a high wall, and no one from the town was allowed to trespass there.

No one. He looked to the edge of the woodland and was astonished to see someone there. At first it was a fleeting glimpse and he thought he had imagined it. But as he kept his eyes on the woodland and half-closed them against the light, he saw it again, he was sure.

He knelt on the cushion of the window seat and peered out, willing the person – if person it was – to show himself. There was a flutter of wind in the meadow between the garden and the wood, and there the figure was again, nearer this time. Then, as suddenly as it had appeared, it seemed to vanish. Then it was back, walking slowly, pensively, toward the house, stopping from time to time and, somehow, fading into the background.

Then William saw the figure clearly and was surprised for, though dressed in trousers, the person was a girl. She must be from the town, he thought, for I have never seen her before. She isn't one of the servant girls; they would never dress like that. She must be from the town and she must have climbed over the estate wall.

The girl paused and put her hands before her eyes, making a kind of frame with her fingers.

What is she doing here? William wondered. And who is she?

He watched the girl make her way slowly across the meadow. She was tall and her fair hair was unloosed and flowed behind her as she walked. She had no bonnet and her clothes were strange, so that he was puzzled. Perhaps she was a gypsy, for he had been told they dressed oddly.

She paused again as if studying the house in front of her. She's coming to call on us, he thought, and was glad. She's pretty, he thought. I would like to know her.

She stopped at the end of the meadow and scrambled up to the rockery. She sat on a large stone, folded her long legs under her, took out a pad of paper from a satchel she carried, and began to draw upon it.

'She's sketching the house,' William said aloud, in surprise, feeling slightly indignant she was doing so without asking permission. He waved to attract her attention. She looked toward him and he tapped on the window, but she paid no heed.

Each time she looked up from her pad to study the house he waved his hand or knocked on the glass but, though he felt she was aware of him, he could not get her to look at him.

William was disturbed and annoyed, and at the same time curious. Who could this girl be who ignored the warning notices, scaled the estate walls, risked punishment for trespass, and now brazenly perched herself in front of the house and, without a by your leave, took a drawing of it?

William felt more intrigued than angry at her intrusion. It was a welcome change, in this time of fear of infection, to have a stranger call. She must be a town dweller, but she looked healthy. Her skin was clear and clean, her clothes, apart from the strangeness of them, decent enough.

And she looked interesting, lively. She's about

my age, thought William, about fourteen, though she is tall, even taller than I.

He watched her now without seeking to attract her attention. She was evidently dissatisfied with her efforts to draw the house, for she tore off a sheet from her pad and thrust it away. William watched as the breeze caught it and blew it toward the house.

William rose from his seat at the window and, with no thought for his mother's warnings about mixing with children from the cholera-stricken town, went through the hall to the door. He would speak to the girl and find out all he could about her. He was fascinated by her.

He opened the door and, as he did, a sheet of paper was blown to his feet. He picked it up and saw it must be the sheet the girl had torn from her pad. It was a half-finished charcoal drawing that showed, recognizably, the shape of the house, but one wing was shown as only partly completed, or perhaps partly destroyed. He stared at it in puzzlement then, closing the door behind him, stepped into the garden with the intention of confronting the girl, of challenging her.

He turned to where she had been sitting. There was no one, no lanky fair-haired girl, no artist, no one. She had vanished into thin air. He looked about him, over the rockery, across the meadow to the woodland. She was not to be seen. He heard a movement behind him and turned sharply, to see one of the ginger farm cats leaping into the grass, hunting.

William stood, puzzled at the girl's disappearance. She had been there a moment ago when he had looked through the window. Now she had gone, and he was immensely disappointed. She

31

must have taken fright, perhaps seen him at the window and run away while he was going to the door.

He looked at the sketch in his hand, an unfinished charcoal drawing. It was there; he was not dreaming.

He was out of the house now – against his mother's wishes – and he felt a sudden relief at being in the open air. He had not meant to disobey her, but here he was. He might as well make the most of his opportunity. He was outside and no one had noticed. His mother would be occupied with the servants and household cares for some time, time enough maybe for him to slip out of the grounds to the railway workings.

He ran round the corner of the house, and keeping behind the hedge that lined the drive, he came to the lodge gates and the house where Bradley the coachman lived. He crept past and was soon out on the road and running toward the town.

FOUR

'You have to remember,' said Mr Richards to his class, 'that Traverton changed totally after the building of the railway in the late eighteen forties. It became a railway town. Everything seemed to be subordinated to the railway. From Traverton lines branched in all directions, connecting Traverton with every major industrial centre in the north. So, it became a centre of locomotive construction and repair, a centre for railway administration. And this changed its life, as well as its appearance.'

He looked at Peggy Donovan and wondered if she was as bored as she seemed. Her attention was certainly not with him.

'Peggy,' he said. He thought he could understand her feelings. She must miss Boston. He had to admit Traverton must seem dull to her. He had once, in a moment of wild extravagance, had a holiday in the USA and paid a brief visit to Boston. He had been excited by the city. No, he would not be surprised if she found Traverton dull.

Peggy was not thinking of Boston, however. Her mind was on the house she had found and which she had tried to sketch. She was annoyed that her efforts had been so imperfect. Art was her best subject and she knew she had sufficient talent to make something beautiful from so picturesque a ruin. But it had defied her, and she could not understand why; she had drawn much more difficult subjects with success.

'Peggy.' Mr Richards's voice penetrated her consciousness and she brought her mind slowly back to the present. She saw he was irritated at her lack of attention and was beginning to fondle his left ear.

'Back with us?' he said, with a hint of sarcasm.

Peggy blushed.

'Where were you?' Mr Richards asked. 'Not Traverton in the eighteen forties, obviously.'

'Adam's Common,' she said, without thinking. 'Why is it called Adam's Common?'

'You've asked that before and I can't tell you. I don't think anyone can.' Mr Richards sounded slightly impatient. 'But you can make it your task to find out. Now back to Traverton as it was last century when the railway came.' He looked about the class, ending up with his eyes on Peggy, making sure she was listening.

'The coming of the railway changed Traverton. The need to provide room for it meant they had to demolish Riverbank and Angel's Meadow, a whole town in itself, a huddle of dwellings by the river, a breeding ground for disease. Riverbank was the centre of a dreadful outbreak of cholera during the epidemic of eighteen forty-eight and forty-nine. Hundreds died down there.'

'Like the Black Death, sir?' said Steven Walsh.

'Not quite as bad as that, but it must have seemed so for the people down by the river. No one really knew what caused the disease or how to stop it from spreading. It was only later, when

34

good sanitation and a pure water supply were provided, that cholera began to die out. But then . . .' He paused to look at Peggy. Her attention seemed to have wandered again.

'Peggy,' he said, plucking his ear.

Peggy smiled, as if she had caught him out.

'Yes, sir?' she said meekly.

'Have you been following?'

'Oh yes, sir. The cholera. Spread by water contamination. A scourge that swept through Asia and Europe and the Americas throughout the nineteenth century.' She smiled again. She had taken a course at home which had dealt with the history of major diseases. She remembered it well and recalled, with sudden horror, some of the descriptions of the onset of the disease.

'Good,' said Mr Richards and continued with his lesson.

It was toward the end of the period that he shifted to another topic. 'Adam's Common,' he announced.

'Why is it called Adam's Common?' said Marion Harper, clumsily mimicking Peggy's American accent.

Mr Richards sharply tugged his ear, glared at Marion and silenced her.

'By now,' he continued, 'it seems to be general knowledge that the Town Council is preparing to sell the common to developers.'

'It's true then?' said Peggy dejectedly.

'I'm afraid so,' he said. 'A public meeting has been called for next month to explain the plans. There's to be a formal signing of the contract with the developers at the meeting. It seems the land is the council's, to do what they want with it. Yes?' he asked as Marion raised her hand.

'I thought the common was there for everyone's enjoyment, common property,' she said.

'So did we all, but who is to say what everyone's enjoyment is?' replied Mr Richards. 'Anyway it's an important issue for the town – and for all of us. So, I think we should give our minds to the arguments, on both sides. I've arranged for two people to come to class next time we meet to discuss it with us – Councillor Brookes, who is chairman of the Planning Committee and of course supports the scheme, and Mr Walter Lyons, a lawyer, who opposes it. We'll have a reasoned discussion – no wild assertions or rumours.'

He looked at Tom Brookes, who grinned at him and said, 'I daren't open my mouth if the old man's here.'

'And,' went on Mr Richards, looking at Peggy, 'no irrelevant questions.'

Peggy shrugged. She thought his remark was uncalled for. It seemed to her important to know why it was called Adam's Common. There must be a reason and someone must know. Who was Adam?

FIVE

William Trafford was not dressed for outdoors or walking over the rough roads of the town. His shoes were light indoor shoes, bright with silver buckles, his pantaloons were made of a fashionable green velvet, and he wore no jacket over his white silk shirt. He did not feel cold, for the day was warm and getting warmer. The sky was blue, almost cloudless, and there was a fresh smell to the country that was pleasing after his enforced stay indoors. He took a deep breath and, when he was sure he was out of range of the house and the lodge, he gave a loud halloo of joy and ran on. It was wonderful to be free from parental restraint.

And there was nothing to worry about; the air was clean and healthy. How could there be danger here? Nevertheless he was aware of the cholera and the savagery with which it had attacked so many towns. It seemed to have been late in reaching Traverton, for only now were tales of its horrors coming out of the streets down by the river, Angel's Meadow, Rowe's Hamlet, Tippett's Backlet, and the rest. William had heard the servants talking among themselves. One of them, a kitchen maid, had family living there and was worried about them, but she had been forbidden to visit them while the cholera was raging.

William knew all this, but it was of no concern to him. If he thought about it at all, he told himself he was immune, and he had no intention anyway of going down to Riverbank.

William was not sure where the construction of the new viaduct was, but when he got to the Great North Road, which skirted the Trafford estate, he turned toward the town. In the distance he could see the tall tower of the parish church. As he walked, he began to have qualms about his mother. If she guessed he had left the house and grounds she would be worried. He hesitated about going on but then thought that, if he hurried, he need not be away from home for more than half an hour, an hour at most. He would find a vantage point from which he could look down to the viaduct; and that would have to satisfy him for the moment.

He came to a row of tall houses, built only ten or twenty years before for the well-to-do professional men of the town. He knew that Mr Lyons, of Lyons, Mather, and Lyons, the family lawyers, lived there, and, afraid he might be seen and recognized, he darted into the shadow of the trees that lined the road.

He thought he saw Mr Lyons at the door of his house, coming down the steps to his carriage, and taking fright, he rapidly turned out of the Parade into a narrow alleyway and ran along it till he felt safe.

He was ashamed of his flight. It showed the guilt he felt at defying his parents – and that made him more ashamed. But his wish to see the viaduct and to catch a glimpse, even, of the engineers at work overcame his unease.

He went on, but a new anxiety seized him. The

38

Parade had been familiar ground, but here at the end of the alleyway, as he turned into a narrow street, there was no landmark he could recognize. The buildings seemed to tumble in upon themselves, leaning at dangerous angles toward each other. A narrow channel ran down the centre of the cobbled street and a brown trickle of water crawled along it, to be dammed here and there by waste of all sorts, straw, decayed stalks of vegetables, and less pleasant refuse.

There were people watching William from the dark doors of the houses, old men and women, shabbily dressed and dirty; William felt embarrassed and angry at their stares. There were children, younger than William, small and ragged, sitting on the steps of the houses. Two boys, dark haired, with dirty faces, seeing William, came up to him and touched his velvet trousers and white shirt. He pushed their hands away and one of them laughed and struck out at William. William dodged aside and slipping, put his foot into the water channel where it had been clogged by an unidentifiable mess.

The boys laughed together and said something to William but he could make no sense of it. He wanted to run away, but pride would not let him show his fear. For he was afraid now – not of the boys, nor the staring faces in the shadows, but of the dirt and the gloom and the smell.

He had been warm when he left home and walked into town; he had been hot when he reached the Parade. Here among these huddled houses, where the sky above was a narrow dark slit, the air, too heavy to circulate, was fetid, close, and oppressive, and he was stifled. He dared not breathe deeply, for the smells were offensive and, he was sure, laden with disease. But he needed to breathe deeply, for the air seemed to hold little goodness in it, nothing to refresh him, nothing to revive his strength.

William felt weak, weak with the strangeness of his surroundings, weak for lack of air, weak with horror. He had not known there were places like this so near to Trafford Court, so different from it, that there were people like these, with their mean, unfriendly looks.

The two boys were following behind; he could hear their footsteps. He wanted to turn and retrace his steps for, as he walked on, the hovels on either side of the passage seemed even more unclean, even more dilapidated and even more crowded with people. But he did not wish to face the boys.

The boys were jeering at him now, he thought, and their calls brought faces to every door, still the same leering faces, hostile.

Then the boys fell silent and William paused. Out of one of the doors came a small sombre procession, following a handcart pushed by a small dark-haired man over the cobbles toward William. He stepped aside to let it pass, and as the cart went by, William saw two small boxes on the cart. He knew them to be coffins. He caught his breath at the thought and watched as the man pushed his load up the hill, with three women and two youths following after.

William was aware now that the street was sloping downward, down to the river, down to the notorious Riverbank. Indeed he must already be, he knew, in Riverbank. He had paused against a wall to let the coffins and the mourners by. Now he looked about him with fear again, but a different fear. His fear was no longer of the people around, but of the circumstances of their lives; his fear was of the odours that clung to everything here, of the dread disease that he knew lurked in the air of this crowded quarter.

He looked at the figures standing in the doorways and saw the pale faces and the tired eyes. They no longer seemed unfriendly, merely indifferent, perhaps slightly curious. He looked for the two boys who, he thought, had taunted him. They were watching him from the distance of a few yards, as if unsure he was of the same kind as themselves. One of them grinned at William, a warm friendly grin, though his teeth were stained and yellow. He came nearer and William spoke.

'Hello,' he said.

' 'Lo' said the boy, and his voice was gruff, and William realized he was older than he looked. He was small and thin and his face, under the dirt, was pale. But his eyes were lively and interested.

'Wotchercalled?' he said, running his words together so that William did not understand him and merely looked puzzled.

'Yer name,' said the boy.

'William,' said William Trafford, of Trafford Court, heir to the Trafford fortune.

'Adam,' said the boy, and studied William with care, looking from the white shirt to the silver-buckled shoes and then looking down at himself, his torn jersey, his ragged trousers, shortened from a long-discarded pair for a much bigger person, and his bare feet.

'Adam,' he repeated. He gestured at his companion, who was standing in the background. 'Zacky,' he said. 'He's soft i'th'head.'

'I'm not,' Zacky said, grinning. He was smaller

41

and thinner than Adam, and even more ragged. He did not approach any nearer to William, keeping well behind his friend, as if frightened of this strange boy.

'What yer doin' 'ere?' said Adam, and again he so slurred his words together that it was a moment before William realized what he had said.

'I'm looking for the railway construction.'

'Railway?' The word seemed to puzzle Adam, then his eyes lit up. 'The workings? I'll tek thee.' He walked on down the street, calling Zacky to come. William followed as well as he could, for Adam was twisting and turning along narrow alleyways that wound in and out among the shacks that here by the river crowded close upon each other. At one turn William lost sight of his guide and found himself in a small cobbled courtyard surrounded by three-storey buildings, with wooden balconies leaning dangerously from the upper floors. There were cries and shrieks coming from one side of the courtyard, sounds of scuffling and quarrelling; a dog came yelping from one of the doors, to be followed by another and another. A stone was hurtled through the air after them and missed the dogs but struck William on the shoulder.

It did not hurt, but he felt assaulted. He was afraid again. The noise, the smell, the dirt in this squalid courtyard choked him, so that he wanted to be sick. He stopped and swallowed the bile that rose to his gullet. An open midden gave off an overpowering stench. He felt sweat on his forehead and under his arms.

His shirt, no longer cleanly white, clung damply to him. He was uncomfortable, inside and out, and he felt alone.

He was not alone; from the balconies around him men and women looked down upon him, pale faces, piercing eyes, once again, he felt, hostile. They called down to him, and their voices echoed and re-echoed in his ears, within his head, booming, resounding, words jumbled together, repeated meaninglessly, until, in desperation, he clasped his hands to his ears to shut out the sound.

The sound was within his head, reverberating; he tried to call out, to command it to stop, but no voice came; he tried to breathe deeply, took great gulps of the foul air, but it seemed no air came. He was drowning, he felt, as surely as if he were in the river itself. He could feel the atmosphere engulfing him, as the water would, and struggled against it, but it was no good; there was no air to feed his lungs, only this sour taste that caught at his throat. He called out and wasn't sure what he had cried. It was a cry for help, as his legs gave way under him and he fell to the cobbled yard.

SIX

Peggy gathered together her sketching materials, pad, charcoal, and a few pastels, and set off to walk through Adam's Common. The house she had found had defied her efforts to draw it before, but she would not give up. Her first glimpse of the house, with its brick-red walls, its tiled roof, its charred timbers, had captivated her. It had shown her a strangely beautiful face, full of magic and mystery, and she was determined to capture that image.

Peggy's mother had shown no surprise when her daughter had said she was getting up early to go sketching. 'Be back in time for school,' she had warned in a sleepy voice, when she heard Peggy moving.

The streets were empty but for one early milk delivery van, and the common was deserted. Peggy came out of the woodland onto the meadow, with its long grass and thistles, and stopped to look at the house. Its mood had changed. The low light of the early sun threw shadows differently from her last visit, and the rockery and the whole front of the house were in shadow, except at one corner, where a glint of reflected light shone from a remnant of glass at an upper window, winking at her. For a moment

Peggy thought there was someone signalling her; but if there was, it was a message she could not understand.

She walked across the meadow in front of the house, trying to determine the best angle to draw it from, but she could not make up her mind. Whenever she stopped to study the house, there was something about it that disturbed her. She had thought it before to be a happy house, even though derelict and half destroyed. But now it was not merely derelict but desolate, a tragic ruin of what it had once been. However she moved, to try to capture it from different viewpoints, it only showed itself as a house of infinite sadness. It was weeping and it made Peggy want to weep with it. She could feel its tears.

She thought she had let her imagination run away with her when she heard the sound of water falling upon the stones in the one-time rockery. Then she heard the patter of rain as the sky darkened and, about her, a storm broke.

She ran for shelter, not back into the woods but onto the porch of the house, and stood huddling against the door. She leaned on it in her anxiety to get away from the rain, and as she did, it yielded behind her and she almost fell through into the darkness of the ruin.

She steadied herself, caught hold of the door-jamb, and slowly turned to look. At first she could make out little, for the gloom was intense; the windows set in the walls were thick with the grime of years and laced with cobwebs. She took a step forward and the floorboards creaked with a noise that sent a shudder along her spine.

Gradually, her eyes became sensitive to the dark and she began to distinguish the sides of the hall, the doors that led from it and the staircase that rose to one side of it.

She stood still, trying to prevent the mood of the house from oppressing her, but there was a sadness about it that she could not deny, that caught hold of her.

Suddenly, a gust of wind slammed the door against the wall and leaves from the porch flurried into the hall. The door swung back and forth in the wind, each time with a grating sound that made her think someone was trying to thrust it to and close her in.

Peggy grasped the door to hold it open and against the force of the wind (if that was what it was) she had difficulty in holding it still.

She looked out to the rockery and the meadow and woodland beyond. The brief storm was passing, the clouds lifted and the rain ceased. She realized time was pressing. The opportunity to make the drawing had passed. She must get home, have breakfast, and get ready for school.

The house would have to wait and, thought Peggy, as she turned back from the wood's edge to look at it, it has waited for centuries, so it will be there when I return.

The sun had risen higher and the shadow moved from the front of the house, but it still seemed sad, and its windows dark and sightless eyes.

She hurried home.

SEVEN

' 'Ere, drink this.'

William heard a voice, faintly, as if from a great
distance, and he felt moisture at his lips. He
opened his eyes to see someone stooping over
him, holding a metal cup to him.

'Water,' said the voice. 'Do yer good.'

He thought he knew the face.

'Adam,' he said as he recognized the boy and
allowed the water to trickle into his mouth
and down his throat. It was warm and acrid to
the taste, not at all like the clear well water they
had at home, but his mouth had been dry and he
was grateful for the drink.

'What yer been doin'?' said Adam, supporting
William as he sat up to drink. 'And what've they
been doin' to you?' He was angry. 'They've
nicked your trousers and your shirt, and your
shoes. Wait 'ere. I'll get 'em for you. Stay with
'im, Zacky, so they don't take 'is drawers as well.'

William heard Adam's footsteps retreating.
Zacky put his thin arm round William's shoulders, holding him as he drank the brackish water.
William looked down at himself. He was almost
naked. While he had been unconscious – how
long, he wondered – he had been stripped of his
clothes. Who had done it, and how?

He shivered; the high buildings around the courtyard threw deep shadow into the corner where he was lying. There was still a sour flavour to his mouth, but he felt better. He sat up and took the cup from Zacky, but he did not want to drink, for the water tasted foul.

'I'm all right,' he said and stood up, unsteadily. He felt awkward, wearing only his drawers, and his feet were bare. His shoes and stockings had been taken too. The cobbles felt hard and they were damp and dirty.

Zacky stared at him. 'Yer all white,' he said and, laughing, looked at his own dirty hands and legs.

There was a shout from one of the balconies and William looked up to see Adam waving a pair of green velvet pantaloons in the air. A woman, with long unkempt hair, was trying to reach them, but Adam threw them down into the courtyard.

'Catch!' he called and, as they fluttered down, Zacky leapt forward and caught them before another woman, as malevolent in appearance as the one above, could grasp them.

'Run,' shouted Adam to Zacky and William. 'Go on. Get moving.' He turned away and scampered off the balcony.

'Come on,' yelled Zacky, and William followed him out of the courtyard. He saw him dart behind some wooden fencing and he went after him. He heard voices, and footsteps running on the cobbles, but no one followed them behind the fence.

William felt black clinging mud at his feet and knew they were on the riverbank. The summer drought had reduced the river to a shallow flow down the middle of the bed. Here at the side the riverbed was thick with slime, yellowish-brown with rotting sewage; gulls rose unwillingly from the debris as Zacky darted through them. He seemed used to walking here and nimbly picked his way over the mud, but William, with the mud oozing over his toes, moved slowly, vainly trying to avoid the evil-looking piles of dirt in his way; in evading one mess he would step into another.

Once one leg sank almost to the knee, so that he was afraid he would be sucked under, but he dragged himself from the squelching sludge and found firmer ground.

Zacky was standing under the arch of a stone bridge that spanned the river here. At the foot of one of the piers the granite base was firm and free of mud. Here Zacky waited and William, thankful to escape the black drag at his feet, joined him.

'Adam'll find us,' said Zacky.

William still felt queasy, and as he looked down and examined himself he felt no better. He was filthy, arms, hands, legs, even his drawers were coated with grey, wet and slithery. He tried to wipe it off, but even though it was drying, it seemed to have a sticky, gummy quality. I'll never be clean again, he thought, and shuddered.

Zacky was peering out from under the bridge. He waved and whistled through his teeth.

'He's here,' he said. 'Adam.' He spoke with admiration as if he knew Adam would always manage to escape from danger.

Adam appeared with William's green velvet pantaloons clutched under one arm. 'You dropped 'em,' he said to Zacky, then to William, ' 'Ere y'are. I saved 'em for you, but you've said good-bye to your shoes and shirt. The arch-cove'll 'ave 'em by now.'

49

William did not understand – only that he could now cover himself a little. He took the trousers and hauled them over his mud-caked legs.

'They're torn,' he said as he drew the waistband tight and saw the cloth of one leg had come apart at the seam.

Adam grinned. 'Old Ma Thackrey didn't want to part with 'em, so I 'ad to tear 'em away from 'er. They're better'n nothin', aren't they?' He sounded belligerent, and William was sorry he had seemed ungrateful and said so.

'Yer a proper toff, aren't you?' said Adam. 'You don't look it now though, I can tell you. Eh, Zacky?'

Zacky grinned and shook his head.

'They'd steal yer wooden leg, if you 'ad one,' said Adam. 'What yer doin' in these parts, any road?'

William wondered now why he had come out. What was he doing here, in this unfamiliar world, so near to his own home, and yet so far from it in every way he could think of? He shook his head as if he did not know the answer.

Then he remembered. He had come out to see where the viaduct was being built, to see the engineers at work.

'The railway,' he said. 'I came to see the building of the railway.'

'Oh aye,' said Adam. 'That's where we were going. Come on then. I'll tek yer there.'

EIGHT

'I'm glad to think you're settling in all right at school,' said Peggy's mother. 'Is it all right now?' She was making sure her daughter's uniform was neat and correct, conforming to school rules. 'Are those right?' she said suspiciously, looking at Peggy's footwear. 'They don't look very suitable.'

'Everybody wears these,' said Peggy, glancing at her casual, bright-coloured shoes. 'Nobody wears brown brogues.'

'If you say so, Peggy, but I don't want you to get into trouble. It's important to make a good impression.'

I don't know why, thought Peggy. They can take me as they find me. But she did. She was glad that most of her classmates now accepted her. Only Marion Harper was still standoffish.

'Don't bother about her,' said one of the other girls. 'She used to be friends with Steven Walsh, till you came.'

'I can't help what Steven does,' said Peggy, but she was sorry Marion was unfriendly, for she would have liked to help in the survey, to do something to help the school win the Trafford Award.

'You'd better find something of your own to do,' Marion had said. 'We mean to win the

Trafford Award, and you can't be much use to us in that.'

'You can keep your survey to yourself, then, and your Trafford Award,' Peggy had said, in a fit of pique, but she was hurt at being excluded.

She enjoyed some things at school. She was good at art, and the teacher – Mr King – was encouraging. She was good at netball, which was new to her; her height gave her an advantage; and she was pleased when she was chosen for one of the school teams. She was annoyed that she wasn't allowed to play football, though, for she was as skilful as any of the boys.

'It's not ladylike,' said Miss Hickman, the elderly games mistress, when she protested.

Peggy did not argue, but at lunch times, when the boys in the third year picked teams to play together, she invited herself to join in and was soon accepted by them.

'You're all right,' Tom Brookes said to her, 'though you are . . .' she thought he was going to say 'a girl', but he didn't. 'You're all right,' he said, 'even if you are a Yank.'

She was accepted and the teachers had ceased to regard her as a stranger from another world. Mr Richards had stopped calling her 'our visitor from America', recognizing that she was here to stay.

Peggy found the social studies lessons fascinating. She still thought downtown Traverton was dull, dirty, and depressing, but its history was interesting. Mr Richards had told them of the building of the railway viaduct in the 1840s and she had gone with the art class to study and draw it. She was proud of the painting she had made. It showed the tall structure graceful against a lowering sky.

'Melodramatic,' Mr King had said, 'but somehow true. Atmospheric. You've talent, Peggy, real talent.'

That had annoyed Marion Harper further because she had, till Peggy's arrival, been regarded as best at art. Her paintings were meticulous, careful, and pretty, and Peggy disliked them. Peggy's drawing of the viaduct was now in Mr Richards's possession; he had admired it and begged the use of it for his lessons with other groups.

'Sign it, Peggy,' he had said when she handed the painting to him. He smiled and added, 'It will double its value.'

She signed it with a flourish and, flustered with pleasure, sat in her seat at the front of the class.

'This is the day,' said Mr Richards, 'when Councillor Brookes and Walter Lyons are coming to discuss the issues arising from the plan to build on the common. They'll be along in a moment. In the meantime let me remind you – if you need reminding – that what happens to the common is of importance to us all. Building there will change the face of the town for good – I mean, forever. Whether it will be for good is another matter. I think you know my views. Yes, Steven?'

'You're against the building plans, I reckon, from what you've said, sir.'

'Yes, at the moment, but I'm willing to listen to the arguments, and to weigh them up fairly.'

'He'll still be against it, then,' a clear whisper came from the back.

Mr Richards began to pluck at his ear lobe. This time, thought Peggy, he really is angry.

He had recovered his composure by the time

Councillor Brookes and the young lawyer Walter Lyons appeared.

Councillor Brookes was not a bit like his son except that each had a large and crooked nose. But, whereas Tom was round-featured with a good-natured smile, his father was thin of face, with small and mean eyes and a fixed and affected smile.

Walter Lyons, the lawyer, was very different. He was short and slight and young in appearance. If he had been lost in a crowd of boys in the school he would not have been noticed; but his face was serious, his forehead lined, as if the problems of each of his clients had left their mark on him. He was nervous at meeting the class, in contrast with Councillor Brookes, whose manner was patronizing and over confident.

Mr Richards introduced the subject and Peggy was surprised that he showed no feeling against the plan to allow development on the common. He merely stated that the council was considering the sale of the land to the developers.

'Not considering,' interrupted the councillor. 'We've already made up our minds.'

The young lawyer looked up angrily and his nervousness seemed to vanish. 'Then what's the public meeting for?' he asked. 'Merely to rubber-stamp your decision?'

'In a manner of speaking, yes,' said Councillor Brookes, unabashed. 'People like to have their say, so we're giving them the chance. I can't see it'll make any difference. There's nothing to be said against the plan, after all.'

'That's why we've invited you both here,' Mr Richards said quickly, seeing, Peggy was sure, the young lawyer's mounting indignation. Mr

54

Richards asked Councillor Brookes to say what benefits he thought the development would bring.

The councillor elaborated on the shortage of good building land, the value of attracting commercial headquarters to the town, the need for modern shopping facilities with car parks. 'It will bring trade to the town, you'll see. We'll put one over on our neighbours.' He looked proudly about the classroom. 'There'll be a stone commemorating it, with the name of Councillor Brookes on it. Something to be proud of.'

Peggy could not believe the man could be so blind as not to see what harm there was in building on Adam's Common. It was an area of great natural beauty, providing a breath of fresh air to the townspeople. She wanted to stand up and proclaim herself a defender of the common, but she could see, as Walter Lyons spoke, that her defence was not needed.

The young lawyer spoke with passionate conviction of the joy that generations of children had found in the common. 'What compensation will this trade, the arid concrete car parks, the towering office blocks, bring for that?' he asked. 'Where will the youngsters go then?'

Councillor Brookes snorted. He had heard these arguments before and defeated them.

'And by what right does the council take this land away from those to whom it was given?' said Walter Lyons.

'It's the council's to do with as it pleases,' Brookes asserted.

'It was given to the council for the people to enjoy, for leisure pursuits, to provide an open space for the well-being of the children of the town,' said the lawyer.

'What evidence is there for that?' smirked Brookes. Peggy saw that he had met this argument before also and knew the strength of his case.

'Tradition,' said Lyons weakly.

'But no written document,' said Brookes, as if that disposed of the case.

'You well know that the archives of the Trafford family went up in flames when the records office and our own office were bombed during the war.'

'You produce some evidence and maybe we'll change our minds, but till then,' said Councillor Brookes, 'there's nothing you can do. So you'd be better attending to your own affairs.'

'It is my affair,' said the lawyer. 'I'm a citizen of Traverton. I walk on the common daily. I played there as a boy and I want any children of mine to play there, wander where they want over it, without interference. And their children too,' he added defiantly.

'Produce the evidence,' challenged Councillor Brookes and looked smugly over the heads of the students to the back row where his son was trying to be inconspicuous.

'Produce the evidence,' he repeated and then he looked ostentatiously at his watch and said, 'I'm a busy man, Mr Richards. I've got a meeting with the developers. If there's nothing else?' He rose and patronizingly thrust out a hand to the lawyer. 'Keep fighting, young man. That's how to get on. But make sure you choose the right cause. This one will do you no good. Good morning, children,' he said and swept from the room.

'Children!' said Peggy under her breath. She looked with sympathy at Mr Lyons. His nervousness had come back and he turned to Mr Richards for help.

'I'd better go too,' he said.

'No, you'd not, Walter,' said Mr Richards. 'We'd like to put questions to you, I imagine.' He looked at his class.

'Is there any chance of finding any evidence to show the common can't be built on?' asked Steven Walsh.

Mr Lyons took time to answer. 'I have a feeling there must be some document somewhere. My family have been lawyers to the Trafford family since 1784 and so we should have had charge of all the documents and deeds. The common was part of the Trafford estate up to 150 years ago. That we know. Later it was handed over to the town, tradition says "for the enjoyment of the people and the well-being of its children." But when our old home and offices on the Parade went up in flames, so did the Trafford papers, and so, we presume, went the deed of transfer.'

Peggy had put up her hand. 'Aren't there any members of the family left? Won't they know if there's any evidence?'

The lawyer seemed surprised at her accent, but smiled and said, 'There's an old lady, the last of the real Traffords, but she only has memories. I've asked her. The old home, Trafford Court, was destroyed by fire some years ago. Perhaps there were papers there, but if so, they've gone now.'

Peggy saw, in her mind, the old house she had tried to draw. She spoke without thinking. 'Is that the house at the far end of the common, beyond the woods?'

Walter Lyons looked surprised. 'It's a ruin now. Do you know it?'

Peggy nodded, but she didn't wish to say more. She wanted to keep the house secret. She had found it and somehow she felt the house and its memories belonged to her and her alone. She did not want to share it, not even with her friend Steven.

'Any more questions?' said Mr Richards. 'Mr Lyons is a busy man too. We shouldn't keep him much longer.'

The lawyer was looking at Peggy. She knew he could see she had a question. But she had been warned against her 'irrelevant' question.

'Well?' said Mr Lyons as Peggy hesitated.

'I wanted to know,' began Peggy, looking at Mr Richards for warning signs, 'I wanted to know why it's called Adam's Common.'

She heard Marion Harper snigger and half turned to confront her, but Mr Lyons was answering her question and taking it seriously. He leaned forward.

'I've wondered that too. It's been known as that ever since I can remember. I'd like to know, and I think it may be important. There must be a good reason for its being called that.'

'Perhaps one of the family was called Adam,' interposed Mr Richards. He too was interested in the problem, Peggy saw, for all his calling it irrelevant.

'No,' said Walter Lyons. 'There's no one. There's no trace of an Adam.'

'Perhaps,' said Tom Brookes, 'it was called Adam's Common after the Garden of Eden.'

Walter Lyons laughed, his nervousness now quite gone. 'That's a bright idea,' he said. 'I expect it seemed like paradise when the citizens were first allowed to use it.' He turned to Peggy. 'But the truth is we've no idea why it's called Adam's Common and I have a feeling that if we

58

knew the answer to that it might lead us to the evidence we need. But . . .' he paused, shrugged his shoulders, and added, 'we've not much time to find out, and I don't know where to look next. I've searched everywhere.'

The bell for the end of school surprised them all. The afternoon had gone quickly. Peggy and Steven found themselves in the company of the young lawyer as they crossed the common.

'Look at it,' said Walter Lyons as they stood together under the oaks. 'Wouldn't it be criminal to destroy all this?'

'What can we do about it?' said Steven.

The lawyer did not answer, but Peggy said, with a confidence that surprised her, 'We'll find a way, you'll see.'

And, as she walked across the grass along the winding paths to home, she felt certain the common would be saved. She did not know how but, as the sun lit the distant woodlands beyond which lay the ruined Trafford Court, she had no doubts.

'You'll see,' she repeated, as the lawyer said goodbye. 'We'll find the answer.'

NINE

'Come on,' said Adam. 'I'll take you to the workings. We can follow the river.'

He spoke in a rush of words all piled on top of each other, but William was beginning to understand his strange manner of speech.

'Come on, slow coach,' said Adam as William reluctantly stepped into the grey ooze. He felt uncomfortable now that the caked mud had dried on his legs. His pantaloons were stiff with it. He looked a sight; his velvet trousers were no longer fashionable green, but grey and filthy. He was covered with dried grey slime, a fit companion for his two friends.

They are my friends, thought William, and was pleased at the notion. They saved me, he said to himself, they recovered my trousers.

He stumbled after them, trying to keep up with them, but it was no use. They were almost as nimble in this clinging dirt as on dry land. It was their element. He called after them and they turned to wait. Then Adam shouted something. 'Look out!' William thought it was.

He turned round, for behind him he heard angry shouts and the sound of wet footsteps slurping through the mud. There were three youths running toward him and, behind them, urging them on, the wild-eyed grey-haired woman who had had William's trousers.

'Get 'em,' she was screaming. 'Get 'em!'

William did not understand, but Adam shouted, 'Come on, Will'm. It's Ma Thackrey's boys. Run for it.'

He ran, or tried to, lifting his feet out of the grip of the mud to reach firmer ground at the edge of the riverbed, but, though the ground was harder here, it was covered with rubble, jagged metal, broken glass, so that progress was more dangerous.

'Over here,' yelled Adam and came to help him.

'Got yer!' said a voice in William's ear and he felt a rough hand at his shoulder. 'Got yer!' An arm was clasped about his throat and he thought he would choke. He spluttered and struck out at his assailant. He could feel him and smell him, but could not turn to see him.

Then he heard a wild cry and felt a body hurl at the youth grasping him. He slipped to the ground and rolled down the riverbank to the edge of the water, with the arm still about his throat, but looser now, so that he was able to take a great gulp of air.

He struck wildly.

'Hey, that's me,' he heard Adam protest. He could just make out the shape of his friend in the flailing mass of arms and legs. There were two others struggling with them in the mud and, though their features and hair and bodies were dripping with river slime, he knew they were Ma Thackrey's boys. He knew now whom to hit, but he had little strength. He still had not fully recovered from his faintness and his legs were weary from trudging through the mud. Except for

61

Adam he would have given up. Except for Adam he would have surrendered his trousers, and his drawers too, for that matter.

Adam's fists were everywhere, and as he struck, he dodged so that for every three or four blows he got home he received only one in return. He was enjoying the scrap, William could tell.

But William was frightened. He could see the eyes of the two Thackrey boys gleaming out of their slime-covered faces, and they were mean and malevolent. He wanted to run, but his legs were heavy; he called for help, but where would help come from? Here in Riverbank, his father had said, the law had no force.

He struck out in desperation and, by accident, landed a blow on his attacker's nose. He felt the jolt and crack as his fist landed. The figure in front of him paused and put a hand to his face. Two dark red channels flowed slowly down the black mud that covered the youth's face. The youth wiped his hand across his face and looked in surprise at the blood.

The other youth had paused too. William and Adam got to their feet and looked at the two Thackreys while, in the background, Zacky sat astride the third Thackrey, holding his face down in the mud.

Farther away, shaking her fists in anger, stood Ma Thackrey, screaming something – words that William did not recognize but which, he knew, conveyed malice and frustration.

The two Thackrey boys retreated slowly as Adam, with silent menace, stepped forward. Adam was small and slight beside them, but there was a fury in him that made the Thackreys admit defeat.

'We'll get yer for this,' spluttered the one with the bloody nose. 'We'll get yer. Those pants were ours.'

'Anyway,' said the other. 'We've got the shoes.' He turned and fled with his brother when Adam darted forward. The third wriggled from under Zacky and, stumbling and slipping, joined his brothers and his mother, who was still shouting curses at them. She turned on her sons and began berating them. Then she cried in her shrill voice, 'Yer'd better watch it. We'll get yer, Adam. We'll get yer, Zack. We'll get yer.'

William, though bruised and weary, felt proud of himself. He had never before been in a fight; he had only met boys of his own age before in the company of his parents on visits to friends and relatives. He had been carefully kept away from boys like Adam and Zacky; he had not even known such boys existed. He had no friends like that – not before. But he had now. He wanted to show Adam and Zacky what he felt about them, but he did not know how to.

Adam was looking at him. His eyes shone out of his dirty face. He had wiped his hands over his face to clear the mud from it, but had only succeeded in smearing it more evenly over his features. But his eyes showed William there was no need to say anything. Adam understood, for his eyes were warm with friendship.

'Yer all right,' said Adam, and William needed no more. 'Come on, let's go to the workings. The Thackreys are done with now.'

He led William along the riverbed. Soon, for they were moving upstream, away from the hovels of Riverbank, the riverbed became cleaner, with less rubbish and filth deposited at its sides, and the water, no longer brown and murky, glistened in the sun. The banks of the river rose higher, the channel narrowed, and the river deepened so that they had to scramble up the side and find a footing on a path that clung to the steep bank.

They turned a bend in the river and William saw it – the beginnings of the viaduct that would bring the railway to Traverton. There were three great columns of stone standing between the riverbanks, rising elegantly to the sky. From where William stood, near the bottom of the bank the pillars looked immense, broad-based in the water but tapering to a slender summit, so slender that it seemed unbelievable that such grace could contain strength enough to support the weight of a bridge and rails, locomotives and carriages.

He stopped to gaze in wonder at the work. He could see tiny figures at the tops of the pillars and others on the sides of the ravine. He had forgotten his new friends in his admiration for the work of the engineers. He was glad he had defied his mother and come out to find the workings.

His mother! What would she think if she could see him now? Would she recognize him? He looked at himself. He was, like Adam and Zacky, covered in river mud, drying now in the sun. He tried to brush it off and pieces of it cracked and flaked and fell away, but it was grey and dirty underneath. No, his mother would not recognize him. When he got home, he must get to the water pump in the stables and wash himself down before she saw him. He did not think how he would explain the loss of his shirt and shoes.

Adam and Zacky too had stopped and were

brushing off the worst of the dirt. If I look any-thing like them, thought William, no one will know me.

'Well,' said Adam. 'D'yer want to go to the workings, or don't yer?'

'Yes,' he said. 'Lead on.'

Adam began to climb up the bank, reaching from one patch of scrub to another. Zacky fol-lowed, as much at ease as his friend, with a foot-ing as safe and agile as a mountain goat. William went after them, slowly, carefully, uncertain, afraid to look back into the ravine. Once a branch he took hold of snapped and he thought he would fall, but he clung to the side and regained his balance and hold. He became more confident as he rose higher. The slope was not as steep as it had seemed below and soon he was within reach of the top. Adam leaned over, stretched an arm out to him and drew him up.

They sat together and looked across the ravine and then, along the bank, to the site of the work-ings. It was only a couple of hundred yards away, and William could see the gangs of men hauling wagons laden with stones or timbers. He saw, apart from the workers, a group of men, frock-coated and tall-hatted, looking over to the other side of the gorge, one of them pointing while the others followed the sweep of his arm.

'That's Joseph Locke,' said William. 'George Stephenson's friend.'

'Who are they when they're at home?' said Adam.

William looked at his friend in surprise. Where had he been that he did not know the names of great engineers?

Then William recognized his father standing

next to Locke and, without thinking, jumped up and ran toward him.

More cautiously, Adam and Zacky followed.

'Hey!' yelled a man, clearly in charge of the unloading of the stone. 'Hey! Clear off!' He yelled at one of the gangers. 'Get those ragamuffins! Clear them off! Catch 'em!'

Two or three of the men stopped work, watched for a moment and then gave chase. William, surprised at such treatment, for he had forgotten his appearance, allowed himself to be taken, but he saw that Adam and Zacky had turned tail and disappeared.

'Adam!' he called. 'Zacky! Come back! It will be all right.'

But there was no answer. He felt himself seized by the arms and was unceremoniously frog-marched to the edge of the workings.

'Go on, young 'un,' said the ganger. 'It's dangerous here. Get back to your mudlarking. There's no pickings for you on this camp.'

William looked the man up and down and assumed the air of authority he had inherited from his father.

'Kindly tell my father I've come to see him.' He had forgotten for the moment that he had been forbidden to leave the house. He was here at the workings and meant to meet the engineers.

'Oh,' said the man, hands on hips and putting on a piping voice in imitation of William's careful cultivated tones. 'Oh, we want to see our father, do we?' And then he added, in gruff unfriendly terms, 'Clear off afore I belt you.'

'I wish to speak with my father,' said William politely. 'Kindly tell him I'm here, my good man,' he added.

'My good man am I? Stop putting it on. Bugger off while you're safe.' The man gave William a push that sent him flying, then turned his back on him.

William picked himself up, and evading the ganger's grasp, ran toward his father. He slithered past one workman, then another, dodging their outstretched arms and reaching the frock-coated gentlemen. They looked at him in surprise and disgust.

'Hello father,' he said and, suddenly exhausted by the efforts of the day, and by a strange weakness that was sweeping through him, he fell unconscious at his father's feet.

'Why,' said Joseph Locke to his companion, 'there's a queer thing. I thought the young urchin called you his father.'

TEN

Young William Trafford was only vaguely aware of being conveyed from the railway workings to a coach and then being taken home. He thought he had seen a man he took to be Joseph Locke bending over him, a broad-faced, red-cheeked man. William had tried to say something but the words would not come. When eventually he was able to speak, he realized that the man bending over him was not the engineer but was Dr Wainwright, their family physician. He was shaking his head, as if in lost hope.

William saw, standing behind the door, the shadowy figure of his father. Then his vision cleared and he saw his father plainly, and his mother, clinging to her husband for support. He had thought she would be angry at his escapade, but there was no anger on her face, only anxiety. She had been weeping, he could tell, and he wondered why.

He tried to raise his head from the pillow, but he had no strength to do it; he opened his mouth to speak but only a croak came forth. He could hear what was being said about him and wanted to show that he understood, but he was too weak and, in the end, too indifferent to do anything but let the words flow past him.

'Cholera, without a doubt,' said the doctor. 'He had somehow got down to Riverbank, you tell me?'

'So we think,' said Mr Trafford.

'It's raging there.' Dr Wainwright paused to take hold of William's wrist. 'His pulse is very weak. He's cold. You must keep him well wrapped up. Change his bedding regularly. It will need it, though he's emptied most of his stomach contents, one way or another.'

'Doctor?' Mrs Trafford was unable to phrase the question she needed answering.

'Who can tell?' said Dr Wainwright, trying by a kindly tone to reassure her, where no reassurance was possible. 'It will take its course. We shall soon know. The cramps will be a sign. If they're too severe – and the vomiting – there's little hope. I'm sorry,' he added, as William's mother drew in her breath. 'It's better you're prepared.'

William wanted to speak but could not. He felt as if he were distanced from the people in this room. They did not belong to him – nor he to them. They were not part of his life. No one, nothing was.

'But, how could it happen? And so quickly?' said Mr Trafford, a man of science puzzled at the inexplicability of the disease.

'We don't know,' said the doctor. 'Bad air? Something in the atmosphere that breeds most quickly in the filthy conditions of places like Riverbank? Who knows? Air? Food? Water? Cholera flourishes, that's all we know. Keep him apart here. We don't want it spreading in your household, now, do we?'

'Is there no hope?' whispered Mr Trafford.

'Hope? There's always hope. I wouldn't be a physician else,' said the doctor. 'He was a healthy boy before. He may pull through. Why not?' He sounded cheerful, but his manner brought little comfort to William's parents.

'He's the only one left to us,' said William's mother.

'Then pray for his recovery and watch over him.'

William heard and, dimly, understood.

ELEVEN

Peggy was still determined to sketch the ruined house, though she had failed so far. She could not understand why nothing had come of her efforts. The viaduct had presented far more difficult problems but she had succeeded with her painting of that. Maybe it was the light that made the subject awkward, she explained to her mother. 'I'll see if the evening sun will make any difference. It will cast other shadows.'

'Don't be too long, Peggy. You don't want to be crossing the common in the dark.'

'I'll be quite safe, Mum. Don't fuss,' she answered.

She collected her sketching materials and set off across Adam's Common. Each time she visited the common now her heart sank at the fear that soon building contractors would be invading it with their grabs and earth movers and mechanical shovels, but each time she told herself it could never happen. Adam's Common surely meant too much to Traverton folk for them to let it be engulfed in a flood of concrete.

The sun drew long shadows on the grass, and when she reached the meadow in front of the house, there were flights of swallows swooping after evening insects.

71

The house was quiet, peaceful, and as beautiful as it had been on the first occasion. Its mood was no longer sad but restful. The sun warmly caught the red of the bricks and the roof tiles. It was a friendly house now.

She settled on the rock where she had sat before and studied the house carefully before putting charcoal to paper. She could see where the fire had take hold, in the west wing. The roof timbers were bare to the sky, blackened and roughened with fire, but time and nature had softened the charred wood with green mossy growth. The east wing seemed less damaged, though the stone above the windows was smoke plumed. There was still glass in some of the windows, fragments only in the west wing but complete panes in the mullioned windows elsewhere.

As she examined the building, trying to understand why she had failed to capture it on paper, she had the feeling that someone within was watching her. The sensation was not at all frightening, for, as she thought the house seemed friendly, so too was the watcher. What was strange was the watching seemed to come from the west wing, where the ruin was greatest, and where the windows seemed most black and sightless.

It was her imagination playing tricks again, she thought. In any case, she had come to draw, not to hunt ghosts, or whatever it was in the house. She expected it was the cat she had seen before, or some other wild creature.

She settled down to her task. She massed in the shape of the building against the light sky, and that was easy enough while she was dealing with the east wing and the centre block, but again the

72

heavily damaged part of the building on the west refused to be drawn.

That was it, she thought, it refuses to be drawn. It's like some city father, some self-important man, sitting for a portrait, wanting only the handsome parts of him to be recorded for posterity, expecting the artist to conceal the blemishes, to paint over the scars and pockmarks.

She smiled at her fancy. The house is not only friendly, but it's vain; it wants only to be remembered for what it was, a warm, lovely and loving family house. And why not? she thought. Why shouldn't it be proud of the beauty it once had? And why shouldn't I try to respect that wish?

She began to work quickly and easily. The east wing took shape beneath her charcoal, and the centre, and the west wing. Before she realized what she had done, she had drawn the west wing unburned, undamaged, with the clean roof lines of the tiles, with windows complete – not a mere reversal of the east wing, but its own self, with individual differences, an extra mullioned window and, on the stone lintel above it, the carving of some shield of arms. Where had the idea for that come from? She did not know, but she no longer had any doubts about her ability to draw the house. It was appearing before her, with the dignity and charm she had first seen, with the beauty too, but no longer with the picturesquely bared beams and jutting timbers. That she had not captured. Her drawing was of the house as it had been before the disaster struck it.

She stopped, exhausted, with the drawing complete before her. She did not know how long she had taken, for time had ceased to have meaning. She was not even conscious of having used her charcoal, but her fingers were stained with it and at her feet lay fragments she had discarded.

She stared at the sketch. There was something magical to it. She stared again. Not only had she drawn the house as it must have been, but, at the door of the house, looking out at her, sketched in a few deft lines, was the figure of a boy. She looked up.

He was there now, standing gazing at her, motionless as in her drawing. Then, as she stood and moved toward him, he moved too, slowly, his steps unsure. She opened her mouth to greet him, to ask him if he was all right, but, as she spoke, he disappeared. She looked about her to see where he had gone.

I imagined it all, she told herself, but when she looked at her drawing, she saw him there, leaning for support against the door. She had caught, in the few lines she had used, something wistful in his gaze.

She looked about her again, hoping to see him, but all there was was a derelict garden, weed-covered, and an ivied ruin.

She carefully placed her drawing between two sheets of her pad, put it in her knapsack, and prepared to go. She looked at the house, aware again (and not merely imagining it, she told herself) that someone was following her movements. She wanted to go to the house to see if the boy was hiding there, but as she stepped forward, the feeling of being watched left her. She realized it was getting late and that the sky in the west was red with the dying sun. She turned away, and in that moment the fragments ·of glass in the windows caught the rays of the sun, and for an instant, she saw the house in flames, a red glow from within. She told herself it was only the reflection of the sun, but she could not dismiss the idea from her mind, and, as she walked through the meadow to the woodland, the dry stalks of grass crackling under her feet seemed to her ears to be the sound of flames consuming the house.

'You've been running,' said her mother when she got home. 'Running scared, it seems. Did something frighten you? Did someone follow you?' She was concerned for her daughter.

'No,' said Peggy. 'It was nothing. I thought it was late.'

'Did you get the drawing you wanted? Can I see it?'

But Peggy kept it to herself. The house was her secret, and so was the drawing.

'It's not finished,' she said, and went to her room.

TWELVE

Peggy walked back over Adam's Common from school slightly irritated with Steven Walsh. He had stayed behind to play football and had not thought of asking her to watch. She had not expected to be allowed to play, for it was a trial game for the school side. She had watched for a few minutes but it only exasperated her to see on the field boys who had not half her skill.

She did not hurry home. She could not hurry across the common; it was made for slow enjoyment, not haste.

'Hello there,' she heard and turned to see the lawyer, Walter Lyons, walking across to his office in the Parade.

'You're the girl who wanted to know why it's called Adam's Common, aren't you?'

'Have you found out?' asked Peggy.

'I'm afraid not, but I've just been to see old Miss Trafford about another matter. I asked her.' He shook his head at Peggy's enquiring glance. 'No, she didn't know either, but she wants to meet you.'

'Me? Why?'

'I told her about my visit to the school. I mentioned your interest. She likes young people, but hardly ever sees any nowadays. She's a very lively old lady, though she is over ninety.'

'Ninety?'

'They live long in these parts. She'll be very disappointed if you don't go to see her. And you never know, she might remember something. Will you come?'

'I don't mind,' said Peggy. She wasn't sure how she would get on with an English lady of over ninety. Why, that must mean she was born when Queen Victoria was still alive, which made the old lady herself almost history.

'I'll leave a message for you at school with Mr Richards,' he said and went on his way.

That evening she settled down quickly to her homework. She always seemed to have plenty, but this evening was worse than ever. On top of maths (which never gave her much trouble) she had French and biology and, she realized, some work for Mr Richards. He had expected her to familiarize herself with the history of Traverton and she had borrowed from the library, *The Story of Traverton*, a book published in 1862, which told its tale from ancient times to the mid-nineteenth century. The text was boring, but there were some interesting illustrations. There was one of the railway's coming to Traverton. It showed the viaduct, nearly completed. In the foreground a group of men stood, consulting plans, while behind them gangs of workmen were busy laying tracks. She admired the skill of the original artist and of the engraver. She wished modern books were illustrated in this fashion.

Then she saw an even more familiar view, 'Trafford Court from the South'. It showed the house, the house she had found, that she had drawn, her secret house, before fire had marred its beauty.

She took out her own sketch and compared it with the engraving. The details were almost identical, with the extra window on the west wing, the carved shield of arms; only the boy in her drawing was missing from the engraving; the rest was as she had drawn it, as she had seen it in her mind's eye.

Peggy looked at her sketch with a feeling of awe. She did not know how it was she had known so clearly what the house was like, but here was proof that the link between her and the house was real. The house had shown itself to her and she had been open to it.

'Peggy.' She heard her mother's voice behind her and had no time to hide her sketch. She wanted to keep it secret still, but her mother had seen it.

'That's a lovely drawing, Peggy.' She saw the book open at the engraving. 'Oh, I see,' she said, slightly disappointed. 'Only a copy. But you've made a good job of it, just the same.'

Peggy angrily closed the book and put her sketch aside. I can't explain, she thought. No one will understand, not even Mum.

THIRTEEN

William Trafford spent his fourteenth birthday alone. There were no friends with him to share the cake and special tidbits that Mrs Murgatroyd, the cook, had prepared.

'We still don't know if it's safe for you to mix with others,' William's mother said. 'And you're not strong enough yet. You'll see your friends when you're better.'

My friends, thought William. Adam and Zacky. Shall I see them when I'm better?

'I am better, Mama,' he said. 'Quite better. I want to go out.'

'Soon, William, but not yet. We'll let you go downstairs today. There's a treat for you.'

They had him taken downstairs, and he had been glad of his mother's support, for he still felt weak. He remembered little of his illness, had no recollection of the agonies of vomiting, the violent cramps, the weakening diarrhoea, but he knew he was lucky to have recovered so well and so quickly.

'Be careful, William. Don't try to do too much. Sit here by the window.' His mother left him in the library, among the books and family papers. It was the room he liked best of all in the house. It was quiet and restful, and from its windows he could see to the rockery, the meadow, and the woods.

He sat in the window seat and stared out. He remembered the last day he had sat there, the day he had gone into town against his mother's wishes; he remembered he had seen a girl sitting sketching. He had found the sketch; he recalled looking at it, holding it in his hand, but he could not remember what he had done with it. He tried to recapture in detail what had happened.

He had looked from the window and seen the girl coming across the meadow.

As she was now.

She was there, the same girl, with her long fair hair flowing loosely about her head, free of ribbons or bonnet; she was wearing a blouse this time, and a short skirt, revealing long legs, legs that had been covered by trousers before. How strangely she dressed!

She behaved as she had before. He lost sight of her for a moment and then, there she was again, scrambling from the meadow to the rockery, settling down on a large stone to study the house.

William was puzzled. He seemed to be living through the same events as before. Would she tear a sheet of paper from her pad and discard it? Would he open the door to retrieve it, and then, in going to find her, would he end up again at Riverbank? And would he meet his friend Adam again? His friend Adam. His friend.

He longed to meet him, and Zacky of course, but there was little chance of that. His parents would watch over him with even more care than before. He would have no chance to slip away and join his friend.

But there was the girl, sitting before the house, unconcerned apparently that she was trespassing. Perhaps she could be his friend.

He waved to her and rapped his knuckles on the window, but though she looked up, she paid no attention to his signals. She was busy drawing the house.

She was working quickly, only rarely glancing at the house for confirmation of detail.

William tried to open the window so that he could lean out and call to her, but it was secured too tightly and he was still weak. He shook the window frame but the girl took no notice, too intent, it seemed, upon her drawing.

Quietly then, so as not to attract his mother's attention, he crept to the door, opened it, and exhausted with the effort, stood leaning against the doorjamb, looking out at the girl, watching her closely as she looked up at the house, then bent again to her sketch.

He wondered how it was progressing and went to look. He hoped she would not mind his curiosity, and, after all, she was on his ground. She did not raise her head to look at him as he approached but continued with her drawing, regarding her work critically, dissatisfied.

He saw she had not yet drawn the west wing. It seemed to be difficult for her. He bent down to take the charcoal from her and rapidly drew in the missing shape.

She did not seem to mind; he wasn't sure she had even noticed.

He felt suddenly faint with weakness. He closed his eyes for a moment, and in that moment the girl had vanished. He was back in the library, sitting at the window, scanning the meadow, searching for signs of her. There was no one, nothing.

Yet, there was something. As he looked, seeking in the deepening shadows for the cause of the movement he had noticed, he saw a dark figure dart out of the wood, scamper across the meadow, and disappear into the dip between the meadow and the rockery.

William thought at first it was an illusion, a trick of the dying light, but, as he watched, a head lifted out of the dip and two eyes peered through the plants of the rockery, then a body scrambled up, over the stones, and as slithery as a serpent, crept through to where the girl had sat and, glancing from side to side like a hunted animal, settled on the rock.

William could not believe his eyes. It was Adam sitting there, his friend Adam, Adam of the mud battle, Adam of Riverbank. William almost yelled his delight but he knew he must avoid drawing the household's attention.

He knocked on the window and was afraid that Adam would be like the girl, unable to hear him, or unwilling to notice him.

But Adam heard him and saw him and, still looking warily about him, ran up to the house and stood outside the library window.

They looked at one another, smiling through the glass. Adam was cleaner than before. He was still barefooted, and wearing the same ragged, cut-down clothing, but his face was clean.

He gestured to William to open the window, but William shook his head to say it was too hard; then Adam beckoned him to come outside, putting his finger to his lips to counsel silence.

William nodded. He left the window seat and

went to the library door and opened it slowly. The heavy wooden door creaked as he pulled it, but no one seemed to have heard, for when he stepped into the hall, the house was quiet, only a distant murmur coming from behind the door that led to the domestic quarters. From upstairs, his mother's drawing room, there was no sound.

He crept past the foot of the main staircase to the passage that led to the side door, uneasily aware of the shifting of the boards as he stepped on them. The effort tired him and he felt a cold sweat clinging to him. When he reached the door, he paused a moment with his hand on the latch, catching his breath. He opened the door an inch or two only, for the hinges had grated noisily.

'Adam,' he whispered. It was now almost dark outside and, through the narrow gap, he could see nothing.

'Adam,' he said again, a little more loudly.

'Will'm,' came a gruff, warm, friendly voice from outside. 'Ow are yer?'

William opened the door wider and at that moment heard a step behind him and saw the flicker of a candle. His mother's voice rose, anxious and angry.

'William! What are you doing? Are you crazed? Oh, William.'

He heard a scuttling outside, Adam running away, he knew, and turned angrily to his mother. But he was too tired, suddenly, to protest and could not resist when his mother's commanding arm led him up the stairs and back to bed.

'I don't know what you were thinking of, William. You're not well enough yet to go out, certainly not into the evening air. There, settle

83

into bed. You'll have plenty of time to go for walks in the grounds when you're better.'

And William was happy to lie back and sleep and, in his dreams, to meet a tall fair-haired girl and a dark, tousle-headed boy. Somehow in his dreams they belonged together.

FOURTEEN

Peggy's father had flown in from Boston. He had
been there visiting his home office, reporting on
the problems of setting up a branch factory in
Traverton.

He answered Peggy's impatient enquiries
about Boston with a smile. 'It's still there,' he
said. 'But I didn't go to see our old home. I didn't
think I'd enjoy it.'

'Quincy Market?' asked his wife.

'Still there, as bright and busy as ever.'

'Boston Common and the Public Garden?'
asked Peggy anxiously.

'They'll never change,' said her father. 'The
street musicians by the common, the swan boats
and the ducks. Just the same.'

And what of Adam's Common here, thought
Peggy. How long will that stay as it is? Her
father was talking now, not of his visit, but of the
branch factory.

'We've been promised land for the factory, at a
very good price, on a new development here.
Looks good.'

'Where's that?' asked his wife.

'There are plans to build a new industrial complex at the south end of the common.'

'The common?' said Peggy's mother. 'Adam's

85

Common?' She sounded as indignant as Peggy felt.

'Why yes,' said Mr Donovan. 'The common. What's wrong with that?'

'It's sacrilege,' said Mrs Donovan. Peggy looked at her mother in surprise. She had not given any hint of her feeling for the common.

'Now, Betsy, my dear,' began Mr Donovan. He only called his wife Betsy when he wanted to wheedle something out of her; usually he called her Elizabeth.

'Don't Betsy me,' said Mrs Donovan, putting vegetable dishes on the table with unnecessary force. 'It's dreadful to think of building factories on the common. What would you think if they threatened to build on Boston Common, I wonder?'

'That's different,' said Mr Donovan, deaf to his wife's strength of feeling.

'Oh?' said Elizabeth Donovan. 'What's different about it?'

Peggy's father was silent, puzzled at his wife's passion. He looked to Peggy for support, but saw no comfort in her.

'Well . . .' he began weakly.

'It's no different,' said Elizabeth Donovan with finality. 'The common here is a glorious place. Every morning, after Peggy's gone to school, I go for a walk there, to breathe the fresh air, to get a taste of nature. I don't know what I'd do without it. I don't know what the rest of the people around here would do without it either.'

'I didn't know you did that, Mum, walked on the common,' said Peggy.

'You don't know all there is to know about me,'

86

said her mother and, turning to her husband, 'nor do you.'

They sat at the table, silently. Mr Donovan, subdued, carefully avoided his wife's accusing eyes.

'Is nobody doing anything about it?' said Peggy's mother suddenly. 'Someone should start a campaign.'

'What about?' said her husband uneasily.

'To save our common, of course.'

She sounds very determined, thought Peggy. She had not often seen her mother in a mood like this. She imagined her rolling up her sleeves for action and leading the women of Traverton in defiance of the council. She smiled to herself at the picture.

'And what are you smiling at, young woman?' her mother said.

'I was thinking,' said Peggy quickly. 'I know a lawyer who's opposed to the scheme, and a teacher at school. There must be lots of others.'

'Then we'll get them together,' said her mother. She turned to her husband. 'There'll be other places for the factory, won't there?'

'Oh yes,' he said. 'We'd already virtually settled on one before this new development was mentioned.'

Peggy's mother exclaimed, 'Do you mean to say there is vacant land, available for industrial development, and they still want to build on Adam's Common? That settles it, Peggy. We'd better start moving.'

'There's not much time,' said Mr Donovan. 'I gather the final settlement meeting is only three weeks away.'

'We'll get your lawyer friend and the others

together tomorrow then, Peggy. They can drop whatever they're doing and come here,' said Mrs Donovan. 'You'll deliver the invitations for me, Peggy.'

'It's no good, Peggy,' said her father when he saw her surprise. 'She's like a whirlwind, your mother, when this mood takes her. You either go along with her or run for your life.'

So the young lawyer, Walter Lyons, Mr Richards from Town School, Steven Walsh's mother, and two women whom her mother had met while walking on the common gathered to consider what could be done.

'It must be saved,' said Mrs Donovan. 'It's such a beautiful place. It would be criminal to let it be destroyed.'

'Our descendants would never forgive us,' said Mrs Walsh. 'Think of all those lovely days we spent on it when we were children.'

'To business, then,' said Walter Lyons.

They got down to planning and met often in the next several days. They proposed to organize a demonstration to coincide with the public meeting the council had called. Peggy painted placards and posters and before long every corner of their house was cluttered with boards bearing slogans. ADAM'S COMMON IS OUR COMMON, said one. Another poster showed two scenes, one an idyllic painting of green trees rising to a cloudless blue sky, the other, grim factory chimneys belching forth smoke, with a black industrial pall hanging over, and, in the foreground, one stunted tree, bare of leaves.

'Pardonable exaggeration,' commented Peggy's father when he saw it. 'But modern factories are not like that.'

'It makes the point,' said his wife, defending Peggy.

There had already been one or two mild letters in the local press, voicing uncertainty about the development. The Common Defence Committee now had a forthright letter published each day. Peggy's posters appeared throughout the town, and soon a local radio station showed interest. Peggy's mother was among those interviewed.

'That was your mother, wasn't it?' said Marion Harper on the day after the broadcast.

'Yes,' said Peggy, ready to take offence.

'She talks good sense, anyway,' said Marion as if surprised that anyone associated with Peggy could talk sense.

Walter Lyons had become, with the other campaigners, a frequent visitor to their house, and one evening, he reminded Peggy of his promise to take her round to see Miss Trafford. 'It will do her good to see a young face,' he argued when Peggy said she was too busy. 'You can't have me breaking my word to an old lady. And she is a dear. You'll like her. We'll make it next Saturday afternoon. She'd like to arrange tea for you, I'm sure.'

On Saturday, Walter Lyons called for her in his bright red sports car. Peggy admired it.

'It's an old friend,' he said. 'But it isn't really me. I'm not the dashing fellow it deserves to have as its owner.'

Indeed he drove in a very restrained way through the town, past long stretches of suburban homes, to the home of Miss Trafford, a solid Victorian house set in a large ill-ordered garden.

'She's not at all well off. Most of the Trafford

89

money went to another branch of the family.'

The lawyer's car, modern and racy, looked incongruous on the drive. They should have arrived, thought Peggy, in a horse-drawn carriage. The steps to the house were wide, but in ill repair. The carriage lamps on either side of the porch were damaged. The house looked old, neglected.

But inside it was cheerful and neat, and the old lady, into whose presence they were shown by an elderly servant, was cheerful and neat as well. She sat in a high-backed chair, erect and alert. Her face was lined, but that and her thin white hair were the only indications of her great age, for her eyes were brisk with interest, her cheeks were red, and her smile welcoming.

'Well,' she said, in a voice that was slightly frail. 'So this is the young American lady who is so interested in Adam's Common. Come here and let me get a good look at you.'

Peggy advanced and Miss Trafford perched a pair of gold-rimmed spectacles on her nose and studied her – at length. Finally she was satisfied and said, 'She's pretty, isn't she? And sensible with it, I've no doubt. Sit here.' She indicated a chair close by her. 'Tell me all about yourself.'

Peggy looked to Walter Lyons. He nodded encouragingly.

'Who you are, where you come from, and why you're interested in Adam's Common,' said the old lady.

Peggy told her, and Miss Trafford listened, only once or twice interrupting when she failed to understand an American word or turn of phrase.

At the end she nodded and turned to the lawyer.

'Bring me that album,' she commanded, and

Walter brought a fat black leather-bound volume from a table in the large bay window.

'Spread it out and open it up,' she said and swung in front of her the shelf of an adjustable table that stood beside her chair.

'Come here, my dear, while I tell you what I know. There's no Adam among the Traffords, that I'm sure of, but there might be some sort of clue.'

She showed Peggy the first pages in the book. Each sheet was covered with sketches, in pencil, or ink, some tinted with watercolours.

'There,' said Miss Trafford, pointing a bony finger at one drawing. 'That's the old Trafford home.' She sighed. 'It was a fine house. It was burned down, you know.'

Peggy looked. It was her house again, her secret house, and it looked exactly as it did in her own sketch, except that there was no boy at the door.

'There's still a lot of it standing,' said Peggy.

'You've seen it?' said Miss Trafford in surprise.

'I made a drawing of it,' said Peggy. 'Just like this.'

The old lady looked closely at Peggy. 'Well, what do you know?' she said and turned over the pages until she came to a photograph. It showed a man sitting stiffly, hands crossed on his lap. His face was set in a hard expression but his eyes were dreamy, as if looking into the past, or, thought Peggy, the future. In spite of the serious lines about his mouth, the man looked kind and thoughtful.

'That's William Trafford,' said the old lady. 'Cousin to my grandfather, Humphrey. That's his drawing of the house. Those were his sketches I showed you. He never married.' She shook her head sadly.

91

'Did you know him?' Peggy asked, without thinking.

'Why no, girl,' the old lady said, with a high-pitched cackling laugh. 'I'm not as old as that. He died well over a hundred years ago.' She turned to Walter Lyons. 'Do I seem as old as that, Walter? Tell me truly. Do I look one hundred and fifty years old?'

The young lawyer pretended to study her and took some time to answer. 'Not quite,' he said. 'Not quite.'

Peggy was indignant. 'You don't look a bit old, no older than my grandmother back in Massachusetts, and she's only seventy.'

'I think you've earned your tea,' said the old lady and rang a handbell beside her.

While Peggy and Walter ate scones and jam and cream and Madeira cake, Miss Trafford talked about her family. 'William's father, Milton Trafford, was responsible for bringing the railway to Traverton. While the other land-owners objected, he made it possible for the line to pass through Trafford land. It spread a long way in those days, the Trafford estate.' She encouraged Peggy to eat more cake. 'It does me good to see a young person enjoying her food. It doesn't mean very much to me, I'm afraid.'

She went on, as Peggy ate. 'They say William frittered away his part of the Trafford fortune, but he was a generous man. He gave money to set up schools and hospitals in the town. It was he who gave over the common.'

'Adam's Common?' said Peggy.

'Adam's Common, they call it. Yes. But I don't know why,' said Miss Trafford.

'You know what the council is planning to do

with it now?' said Walter Lyons gently.

'Yes,' said Miss Trafford. 'And I don't think William would have approved. But I don't know what can be done about it.'

'Some of us are trying to do something,' said Walter. 'But our case doesn't seem strong enough. I wish you could find, somewhere among your family possessions, something to show William's intentions.'

He looked at Miss Trafford, but she only shook her head. She looks tired, Peggy thought, ready to sleep. Her eyes were closing drowsily and her attention was drifting. Walter beckoned to Peggy and they crept out.

'She always makes a special effort for visitors. Isn't she a marvellous old lady?' he said.

Yes, she is, thought Peggy, but she was disappointed that Miss Trafford could give no explanation of why the common was known as Adam's Common. And, as she was driven home, she began to feel a sense of defeat. Where now could she turn for help in her quest?

FIFTEEN

With each day William felt his strength returning, so that he was impatient with the way his mother fussed over him. She was so unwilling to let William out of her sight that he was moved to protest.

'But,' she answered, 'you deceived me last time when you crept out to town. That's where you caught your sickness. Please, William, we don't want to go through all that again.' She took his hand and gently stroked it.

'Oh, Mother,' he said, exasperated. 'I promise I shan't go there again.'

'Can I trust you?'

'I only want to walk in the garden, into the meadow and the woods, to get some fresh air.'

'It can't do the boy any harm,' William's father said.

'If you give me your solemn promise not to go out of the grounds,' said his mother.

'Honest,' said William.

So, with his mother's eyes uneasily watching him, William went into the garden. At first his legs felt weak under him, and after a few steps he was glad to sit on the large rock at the end of the rockery. His mother came out to tend the plants there and he was happy to rest and watch her as she knelt to weed the bed.

It was afternoon, in late September, and the sun shone on the house front, giving the red bricks a warmth that made the house friendly, welcoming. Inside it had seemed like a prison to him, but now he saw it as it was, peaceful and comfortable. In the distance, beyond the gable, he could see the buildings of the home farm and knew that, beyond that, stretched Trafford land for miles upon miles, and all one day to be his. He knew he ought to think himself lucky to be born to such wealth but there was something missing from his good fortune. He felt vaguely dissatisfied; something was missing and he could not think what it was.

Then behind him, he heard a surreptitious 'Psst!' and he knew what it was he was lacking – his friend Adam. That was what was missing. He turned slowly, so as not to alert his mother, and looked to where the noise had come from. There was the meadow, carpeted with field mushrooms, and beyond it the woodland. He could see no one. He had imagined the sound, after all.

Then he heard it again, near to him, and he realized it came from the ha-ha, the ditch between the garden and the meadow. He got up from the stone and his mother looked up sharply.

'Where are you going?' she asked.

'Nowhere. Just exercising my legs.'

She seemed satisfied and returned to her plants. William stretched his arms and strolled nonchalantly toward the edge of the garden, until he was standing close to the ha-ha.

'Psst!' he heard again and he looked down. Adam was sitting below him, hidden from view of

95

the house. His face broke into a wide grin and he held his fist out, thumb up in sign of triumph.

William put his finger to his lips to warn Adam to silence and turned to look at his mother. She was sitting back on her heels, her black skirt around her, intent upon the rockery.

'I'm going over to the woods,' he called to her.

'Not too far,' she said. 'You're not strong enough yet.'

'I'm all right,' he answered, and he slid into the ha-ha and stepped into the meadow. He gestured to Adam that he was going to the wood, and whistling casually, he walked slowly over to the trees. He did not hear Adam move, but as soon as he reached the wood, Adam was beside him.

They stood in the shadows, looking at each other and grinning. There was no need for either of them to speak. William saw that Adam was as pleased as he was that they were together again.

' 'Ow are you then?' said Adam. 'All right?'

William nodded.

'I heard you were bad. Like to die,' said Adam. 'The cholera they calls it.'

'Yes,' said William.

'Zacky died of it.'

'Oh.'

'And my young brother.'

'I'm sorry.'

'And two of them Thackrey boys. Remember them?'

'I remember,' said William.

'I was feared for you,' said Adam. 'Thought you might be a goner.'

'No, I wasn't,' said William.

'I can see that,' said Adam, laughing. 'You're 'ere, aren't you?'

And William suddenly felt how lucky he was to be here alive, well, and with his friend.

'I've come lots of times,' said Adam, 'waiting for you. Nearly got caught once.'

William heard his mother calling. 'William. William.' And in her voice there was anxiety.

'She's after you,' said Adam.

'William!' she called, rising concern in her voice.

'I'd better be off,' said Adam.

'You'll come again?' asked William.

'I'll be back, Will'm, never fear.' And almost before William was aware, Adam had slipped away and was lost to sight.

'Coming, Mother,' called William and stepped from the shadow of the trees into the meadow.

So, almost every day at some time, during the next month, Adam would arrive. William would watch out for him from the library window, which had the best view over to the woods. And toward the evening usually, as the sun was beginning to set, William would make out a dark figure in the trees, barely visible unless one were watching eagerly, as William was.

William would call to his mother, 'I'm going for a stroll,' and would leave the house by the side door. His mother, it seemed, had ceased to worry, for, with every day that passed, he got stronger, his cheeks recovered their colour, and he came back from his evening walk cheerful and refreshed.

William was sad to be deceiving his mother but he knew she would not understand his friendship with Adam. He knew what his mother thought of the town children. 'Thieves and street urchins, every one of them. And have you seen how filthy they are? They've no pride in themselves. Godless creatures. Someone should do something about them.'

When she spoke like this, William's father would protest, mildly, that they couldn't help themselves.

'That's what I mean,' said William's mother. 'They've no wish to help themselves. They're mean spirited, low, filthy criminals, every one.'

William wanted to deny her charge. He knew Adam was none of these things. But he dared not open his mouth. He could never explain his friendship to his mother. And he did not think his father would approve.

So he gave his parents the impression that his evening strolls were for the sake of the fresh air and the mild exercise. Adam was always waiting for him under the same tree, a gnarled and ancient oak, heavy with acorns. Adam would sit there quietly waiting, cross legged and serene, so unlike the Adam William had first met, the busy restless boy who had fought in the mud.

They did not speak much when they were together. Adam would always ask how William fared, as if it was his fault that William had contracted cholera (as indeed it may have been, since it was Adam who had given him the drink of water that carried the disease, though neither they, nor anyone else at the time, knew of the connection).

Adam seemed content to sit beside William in the woodland, merely enjoying his company. But once, as they heard a bird singing lyrically in a nearby tree, Adam softly enquired what it was.

'A bird,' said William.

'I knows that,' whispered Adam. 'What sort of bird?'

William could not say, but he enquired at home, describing and mimicking the sound, and Cousins, the head keeper on the estate, identified it as a nightingale.

They heard it again the following night.

'It's a nightingale,' said William.

'It's beautiful,' said Adam. ' 'Tis rare and beautiful.' He seemed to feel awe at the sound and kept still, listening to the music, as if he were privileged to be present.

From then on William found it impossible to satisfy Adam's curiosity about nature. There was nothing that escaped his notice, the most insignificant flower under the trees, the hidden bird's nest, the droppings of rabbits; he saw everything, and was curious about everything, so that William left him primed with questions to which Adam demanded answers. And William sought the answers from his mother (who knew a good deal about the flowers of the garden and nothing about the flowers of the woodland and meadow), from his father (who was amused at William's newfound delight in nature), and from Cousins (who was best informed).

William and Adam began to explore the whole of the estate between the Trafford house and the point where the estate jutted into the town. Adam showed William where it was that he scaled the wall each evening. He tried to persuade William to climb back over it and go with him down to Riverbank, but William's memories of that horror were too vivid, and his promise to his mother too solemn, for him to yield to Adam.

He watched Adam mount the wall and heard him land in a rustle of leaves on the other side. He would call, 'Goodbye, Adam,' and would hear a whistle from his friend to indicate a safe landing.

William would turn then for home, his mind filled with the questions Adam had posed, and ashamed of himself that he, living among these things, had taken the wonders of nature for granted, while Adam, brought up in the narrow streets and crowded hovels of Riverbank, was alive to every movement of a wild thing, noticing even the smallest change in the hedgerows, seeing the approach of autumn, and the reddening foliage with delight. With Adam beside him, William's eyes were opened and new pleasures made manifest, and as a result, their friendship deepened and William lived each day for the joy of meeting Adam in the evening.

There were many times when he wanted to tell his parents about his friend, but he kept silent. They never asked him how it was he had arrived at the railway workings in the state he was in, and he had not told them.

They would not understand Adam; they would not be able to see why he preferred his company to that of his cousin Humphrey. So he kept silent, guarding his secret friendship. It felt more precious because it was secret.

He was always afraid that an evening would come without Adam's being there and once or twice this happened, but Adam arrived the next day, unperturbed, offering no explanation for his absence of the night before.

William could not keep his pleasure in his friend entirely to himself; it was too fine an experience to be hidden altogether. He started to keep a diary. His first entry read, 'Today, Saturday, 27th October, 1849, Adam showed me a nest he had found. It was deserted so we did no harm by looking at it. I had walked past the place often before and had not seen it, but Adam saw it. There were some downy feathers still left in it. Adam wanted to know what bird had nested there. I shall ask Cousins'. The next day he wrote, 'Cousins says it will be a blackbird's nest'.

William kept his diary in the library, hiding it behind the volumes of family papers. He did not write a great deal in it, just enough to record his friendship, just enough to feel he was bringing Adam into the house. If only, he thought, I could bring him into the house. He told himself, one day I will; one day, when all this is mine, Adam will be able to enjoy it with me.

'You should make friends with your cousin Humphrey,' said his mother once. 'He's a nice boy.'

'All right,' said William passively, but to himself he said, I have a friend, Adam, and I need no other.

He would sit at the library window in the day, hoping time would pass quickly till the hour when he would see Adam's shadowy figure among the trees, and sometimes he would see, suddenly appearing as if from nowhere, the girl he had seen before, the girl with the strange clothing and the long fair hair. She never stayed long, and he was never sure when she came or when she went. One moment she was there and the next she was gone. She would appear again, nearer the house, quite unconcerned, it seemed, that she was trespassing.

He thought that once he had spoken to her and, though she had not replied, she seemed to understand. He felt she was his friend too, and Adam's in some strange way, for now it was when he was

101

thinking most of Adam that the girl would appear.

There she was again. This time she did not seem to have brought her sketching pad with her, and she was dressed differently, in a bright cotton frock, with a ribbon tied round her forehead drawing her hair back.

She is pretty, he thought.

She's coming toward the house. She's coming to call. He was surprised at this. He waited for the bell to sound, and for one of the servants to go to answer it. He thought he heard the door creak and went out of the library and to the side door. It was standing open, but there was no sign of the girl. He looked into the garden. She had gone. She had intended to come to the house, he was certain, but she must have changed her mind.

It was the wind that had blown the door open, he decided, and indeed he felt a cold sweep of air pass him along the corridor. The curtains at the hall window quivered with the passing of the breeze. He heard the floorboards creak as if someone were cautiously moving along them, but there was no one. From the kitchen quarters he heard a door open and a giggle from one of the scullery maids, the sharp voice of Mrs Murgatroyd rebuking her, and the silence that followed.

He moved back to the foot of the staircase and looked up it. The stairs beyond the curve were lost in shadow, the breeze from the door set the chandelier swinging slightly, almost as if someone had reached to touch it. His imagination was seizing him with strange fancies.

Someone seemed to clutch at his arm for support. 'Is that you?' he said, knowing it was the girl he had seen, but the hand had gone, though the warmth of her touch was still present.

'Please,' he said. 'I have something to tell you.'
Here was someone he could tell about Adam. She
would not betray him. It was important to him to
meet her, to speak to her, but, as he hesitated, his
attention was caught by a whiff of lemon from the
kitchen; Mrs Murgatroyd must be making his
favourite pudding. And in that moment the girl
had gone once more.

SIXTEEN

Peggy's curiosity about Trafford Court was increased by her visit to old Miss Trafford. After Walter Lyons brought her home, she had a quick wash and told her mother she was going for a walk.

'Don't be too long,' said her mother. 'I want you to help with some more placards.'

'I'll only be half an hour or so,' Peggy answered and hurried out toward the common. She thought she heard a shout behind her but paid no attention. She was going to look at the house, perhaps explore it, certainly look around its grounds, satisfy herself. Although she was not quite sure what she had to satisfy herself about. She was not at all sure what she meant to do, but the house had become significant to her, not now as the subject of a painting but in some other way, which she could not understand.

I'm being fanciful, she told herself, but the house is the only connection we have with William Trafford, who owned the common, so there might be some secret there that I could find.

Peggy Donovan was not the sort of girl to have flights of fancy – or so she told herself. She was a very ordinary person, she thought, except for her skill at drawing and painting. But here she was, seeing significance in an old house, a house that wasn't even habitable.

She thought again she heard a shout behind her, but ignored it and hurried on. She wanted to get to the house before dusk because she did not like the idea of wandering about in the dark, and she had not brought her flashlight with her.

There it was, with the sun reflecting from the shattered glass of its windows, lonely, secret, and romantic. She did not hesitate but went up to the house, to the side door. The porch was cluttered with leaves, and as her feet parted them she saw a paper, the sketch she had discarded. How had she missed it before, she wondered, as she picked it up.

She pushed the door. It swung open noisily, with a groaning croak that would have startled any occupants, if there had been any. She stood at the entrance to allow her eyes to get used to the gloom within. A flurry of wind behind her sent some of the leaves from the porch of the house scuttling ahead of her like so many wild creatures, startling her with their dry scampering sound.

The house smelled musty but, for a moment, she caught a faint wafting smell of lemons. She brushed at a spider's web that caught at her face and she felt a tickling at her ear. She put her hand up and felt a spider crawling about her face.

She could see the staircase leading from the hall. She looked up at the ceiling, once ornate with plaster scrolls but now showing great gaps, broken laths and crumbling plaster. There was a slithering sound in the ceiling above and she felt as if sharp eyes were following her movements.

She stood looking around her, conscious of the

decay and ruin that had come to this once lovely home. The beauty she had seen from outside was only a shell, she realized; inside, fire had burned out its heart, and what fire had failed to destroy, time was now working on.

It was sad to see it. She could feel something of the old charm of the house, the wide stone staircase with its sweep upstairs, a corner of panelling still intact, though smoke-blackened, a spacious feel to the hall. Now more used to the gloom, she could pick out doors leading to other parts of the house, but the way to them was barred by fallen beams; only the path to the stairs was clear.

She went over. The stone stairs had resisted the fire. In places the balustrade and rails still stood, but the banister shook unsteadily as she put her hand to it. She put one foot on the bottom step, then saw, as she looked up, a patch of dark sky. A shape swooped past her and she recoiled from it, caught with fear.

It's only a bat, she told herself, and nothing to be afraid of, but she could not convince herself. She stepped back into the hall, tripped over some clutter at the foot of the stairs, and put out a hand to prevent herself falling. Something, or someone, steadied her. She felt a touch.

'Who is it?' she said. 'What do you want?' She did not feel frightened and wondered how she could feel so self-possessed when a moment ago she had recoiled from fear at a bat.

'Who's there?' she asked and thought she heard a murmur, a voice trying to break through a barrier between them, a voice distant yet near.

He wants to tell me something, but I cannot hear him, she told herself, and was impatient at her helplessness to understand.

She knew it was the boy she had drawn. He was trying to reach out to her and she stretched out her hand, wanting to grasp him, but instead she found only the clinging threads of a cobweb and drew her hand back in distaste.

Something swooped near and again unreasoning fear of the bats took hold and she decided daylight was better for exploring.

She retreated to the door, but the echo of a voice seemed to call to her to plead to her to stay. 'Listen,' it seemed to say. 'Listen.' She thought it must be the wind stirring the dead leaves at the door and she turned away.

It was dark outside. She had not realized how long she had spent in the house looking at the desolation there. Over the trees a sliver of new moon appeared.

I must get home, she told herself, knowing that her mother would be concerned. She rushed across the meadow and paused at the wood's edge to look back at the house. It was now a silhouette against the darkened sky, black and forbidding. She hastened through the woods away from it and crossed the common to home.

Steven Walsh was at the end of the road. It seemed he had been waiting for her.

'Where on earth did you get to?' he said. 'I called after you and followed you across the common, but you disappeared.'

She wished now he had been with her. Perhaps if he had, she would not have retreated in fear. Maybe next time she would take him with her and show him the house. Maybe she would admit him to the secret, though she felt it was up to her to discover what the house, and the boy, had to tell her; no one else could help with that.

SEVENTEEN

The campaign of the Common Defence Committee was gaining strength. Public concern had been aroused and Peggy's mother was pleased with the way she was greeted in the town. She found herself making lots of new friends. Strangers, recognizing her (to her surprise) from a photograph that had appeared in the local paper, approached her in the street to wish her well, and Peggy, who went shopping with her at the weekend, was proud of the way she was welcomed wherever she went.

'They only needed a spark to set them alight,' said Mrs Donovan to her husband. 'No one will be able to stop us now.'

'Watch out for fireworks,' said Mr Donovan. He pretended to be amused at his wife's involvement in the campaign, but he was secretly proud of her, and was sorry that his position with his company made it difficult for him to support her openly.

Peggy was kept busy designing and painting posters for the demonstration and had little time for anything else. She was sorry she could do nothing to help in the work for the Trafford Award and hoped, in spite of Marion's awkwardness with her, that her group would win the award for the school. Peggy was so busy that for a time she even forgot her obsession with the old house.

The campaign had been so successful that the council had been forced to recognize public concern and, to counter popular feeling, had made minor modifications to their plans and had had an architect's model prepared to prettify the development.

The members of the committee were invited to view the model. Peggy accompanied them to the council offices, where Councillor Brookes met them.

'Ah,' he said breezily, but not concealing his hostility, 'so these are the people who are trying to teach us our business.'

Peggy felt indignant and saw her mother flush with anger, but Walter Lyons made a gesture of restraint.

They leaned over the model.

'There, you see,' said Councillor Brookes, flourishing a hand at the neatly constructed blocks and the model trees dotted here and there between them. 'You see, all the green is not lost. We're not blind to conservation, not us. There's a square there, with a fountain.' He pointed to a tiny piece of mirrored glass in a court among high surrounding blocks. 'And here, there's a park for the office workers to stroll in.' He indicated some small square patches of green cloth, representing a concession to nature.

It must be, judged Peggy from the scale of the model, no more than thirty yards by forty, a tiny oasis in a desert of concrete. A model tree stood forlornly in the centre of the green patches.

'And here,' said Councillor Brookes proudly,

'now here is something the kiddies will like.' He looked patronizingly at Peggy and she shuddered. She felt her mother's hand on her arm, hinting to her to keep her temper.

'And what's that?' asked Peggy's mother, in a calm cold voice.

'Ah, an aviary,' said Councillor Brookes.

Mrs Donovan looked down at the model.

'A birdcage you mean,' she said.

Councillor Brookes looked at her. Her tone must have warned him of danger. He hurried on. 'A shopping complex with plenty of space for customers' cars, and loading areas, restaurants – we could do with some good eating places around here – offices for all the big companies we hope to attract, a coach station for the additional traffic we expect to bring in.' His speech was rapid, one item followed another to prevent his being interrupted. 'That's Brookes Way,' he said with smug satisfaction. 'That broad road running through.'

'Where's Adam's Common?' Peggy interrupted sharply, unable to contain herself any longer. 'Where's Adam's Common gone?'

'Adam's Common?' Councillor Brookes was nonplussed.

'You've not only taken the common away, you're even getting rid of the name.' She felt near to tears – tears of anger and frustration. 'You don't care, do you?'

She could not bear to stay. She turned her back on them all, and on the hated model, and ran from the Town Hall toward the common.

She had been more disturbed by the sight of

110

the model than she cared to admit. She had not realized that the grass, the woodland, and the hedgerows, the meandering paths, would all disappear, that the common would be so violated.

She now felt she must spend every free moment there, making herself familiar with its every corner, every secret place. And there were scores, hundreds, of such places. It was wild, unordered, where nature could run riot, where birds nested and grew and fed on seeding grasses and hedgerow fruit, where butterflies abounded, where squirrels foraged for acorns and beechnuts, where pine cones fell, and opened and shut with the weather, where field mice scampered, and owls hunted.

She had once seen a pair of buzzards and wondered if they perhaps nested in the trees on the far edge of the common. She saw magpies, goldfinches, and thrushes. She thought, with horror, of the 'aviary' of Councillor Brookes. He would cage all the wild creatures if he could, she thought. And he would cage the people too, trap them into his blocks of offices, imprison them behind desks and tills, marshal them into queues, herd them into car parks.

She shuddered and sought comfort under the trees, wandering along the paths, following them wherever they might lead, breathing the fresh air, here scented with pines, there with wild thyme. Each corner of the common had something new, some precious magic to enchant her.

And it was all to go.

'It can't go,' she said, and realized she had spoken aloud when a wood pigeon, startled at her intrusion, flew along the path in front of her.

111

'It can't go,' she called, and the sound of her voice was lost in the trees. 'It won't happen,' she said softly to herself. 'Adam's Common will remain as it is, as it has been. It will always be Adam's Common, always.'

EIGHTEEN

As the days shortened, it sometimes seemed to William that Adam was not coming, but then he would catch a movement over on the edge of the wood, a sign that his friend had arrived. He would slip out of the house and run across the meadow, hoping his parents would be too busy with their own affairs to bother him.

'He's a fine boy,' he overheard his mother saying to his father, as he crept past.

'Fit enough to get down to his schooling again,' said Mr Trafford. 'He's had long enough to get over it. He needs more than a tutor now, my dear. You'll have to give him up. We'll send him away. He needs that.'

William did not wait to hear his mother's answer but stepped quietly to the side door and slipped into the dark.

'Thought you weren't coming,' said Adam. He led the way stealthily back into the wood to a remote corner they had not investigated before.

'What is it?' whispered William.

'You'll see,' said Adam in the same soft voice.

'Ssh . . .' he said. He knelt down and William knelt beside him. He could not see why they had come. Before them, in a slight clearing among the trees, the ground was uneven, a dip, a mound, and another hollow. He could see nothing but tree trunks, heaps of fallen leaves, a few broken boughs.

He was about to move when Adam gripped his arm. He stayed motionless, hardly daring to breathe. In front of them, from behind the mound, had emerged a shambling creature, grey and black and white. It cautiously snuffled among the leaves, making an odd snorting noise from time to time.

'What is it?' whispered Adam.

'A badger,' said William, raising his voice in his excitement. He had never seen a live badger before, only a dead boar that Cousins had once shown him.

'Ssh . . .' said Adam crossly. 'You've startled him.' The badger had looked up, its snout quivering in the air. It caught wind of them, it seemed, for after a moment it shuffled back, away from them, and was lost to sight.

'I'm sorry,' said William.

'It's all right,' said Adam. 'We saw 'im, di'n't we?'

They waited in the hope the animal would reappear but, though they heard noises about them, they saw nothing more, and eventually, satisfied with their vigil, they returned to the path that led back to the meadow.

How can I tell him, thought William, that I am to be sent away? How can I leave him? I've no friend like Adam, never have had, and never will have. I cannot leave him. I shall have to persuade my parents to let me go to school in the town. There must be somewhere where I could learn mechanics and geology and the other things I shall need to know to be a railway engineer.

He looked at Adam. In the dark he could not see his rags, nor his bare feet. He could see only a dark slight figure and the pale oval of his face. He had never thought how different the two of them were, and how strange it was for them to have become such good friends. He took it for granted that they would always be able to meet, always be able to walk the estate, always be close to each other.

Sometimes William wanted to ask Adam about his family, but he never did, and Adam did not ask him about his parents. They accepted each other without question, and had done so from the beginning.

'I'd better go,' he said when, across the meadow, he saw a light twinkling at the side door, showing a servant coming to look for him.

'See you tomorrow,' he said.

'Tomorrow,' said Adam and disappeared among the trees.

NINETEEN

There was a meeting of the Common Defence
Committee in progress when Peggy got home
from her exploration of the common. The feeling
of the members was gloomy, and even Peggy's
mother was despondent.

Walter Lyons had reported that he had failed
to find evidence that there had been any
restrictions on the use of the common when it had
been donated to the council. Every record had
been searched. The few remaining family papers
had been examined and re-examined. There was
nothing to cast doubt on the council's claim that
they could do whatever they wanted with the
common. There was nothing legally to prevent
the council from handing the common over to
the developers.

'I hate to admit defeat,' said Peggy's mother.

'So do we all,' said Walter. 'But what can we
do?'

'We can continue to make things uncomfortable for the council,' said Mrs Donovan. 'There's
a lot of support for us. Brookes and his friends
can't ignore that.'

Walter shook his head sorrowfully. 'It's hard
evidence we need, and there seems little hope of
that.'

Peggy was certain that the secret lay in the name of the common. Why Adam? Who had he been?

She sat in her room thinking of the common and the people associated with it. She took out her sketch of the house and wondered at the skill with which her hand had drawn the house – not as it appeared now, a sad relic, but as it had been. As it had been in William Trafford's time. As it had been when William Trafford himself had drawn it, in the sketch Miss Trafford had shown her. She knew then where her skill had come from. Another hand had been guiding hers. It was that hand, she felt, that had drawn the figure of the boy. There was something William Trafford had to tell her. He has tried to speak to me already, she told herself, and I did not listen.

She fell asleep, wondering about the boy at the door, and what it was he wanted to say. Throughout her dreams, she heard, as a constant refrain, the name Adam. 'Adam,' she heard. 'Wander where you will. It's yours.'

The next day, Sunday, she decided she would go to see old Miss Trafford again. After all, she was the last link with the family; she might remember something. She caught a bus to the other side of town and found her way to the Victorian house where the old lady lived. The elderly servant recognized her and showed no surprise at Peggy's request to see Miss Trafford. It was almost as if she expected Peggy to return.

'She'll be glad to see you. A young face does an old body the world of good.' She showed Peggy into Miss Trafford's room.

'Your young friend,' she announced and left them.

Miss Trafford was sitting as before in her high-backed chair; the album she had shown to Peggy was on the table in front of her. She looked up from it.

'It brings back memories,' she said. She doesn't seem surprised that I have come to see her, either, thought Peggy.

'Come along, my dear. Stand here by me so I can show you. And I've found something else that will interest you. I didn't know I had it. Over there.' She pointed to a large flat-topped desk at the side of the room. 'In the drawer on the right. It's a secret drawer. There's a spring underneath. That's right,' she said, as Peggy put her hand under the flat top of the desk and released a catch, so that the top drawer could be opened.

'I'd forgotten all about it. I'm like that,' she said brightly. 'Some days I forget my own name. But I've remembered yours. Peggy Donovan, isn't it? And you're interested in someone called Adam, aren't you?'

Her bright eyes looked sharply at Peggy. Today the old lady's voice was strong.

'Adam,' she repeated. 'I said there wasn't an Adam among the Traffords, nor was there. But you'll find mention there of one.' She pointed a bony finger at the small exercise book Peggy saw in the drawer. 'Take it out, dear. Treat it gently. It's very old. You have to treat old things gently, like me.' She laughed, a thin high laugh, full of mischief and delight.

Peggy held the book in her hands. Its grey cover was dog-eared at the corners; the sheets inside felt brittle, old.

She looked at Miss Trafford for explanation.

'Bring it over here, Peggy.'

Peggy took it to Miss Trafford, who held it before her for a moment, in a dreamlike way, before speaking.

'It's strange how holding it makes me feel close to my family.' She paused. 'To the past. To the people I never knew, who never knew me.'

Peggy was silent, watching the old woman as her hands, skin yellow and brittle as the paper, turned the pages of the book. Then she seemed suddenly to tire and her eyes looked beyond Peggy, so that, as the silence stretched, Peggy thought old Miss Trafford had forgotten she was there. Then she spoke.

'Take the book over there, my dear, by the light. You'll see what I mean.' She handed the thin book to Peggy and said, 'Elspeth will bring us some tea if you ring when you're ready for it.' She closed her eyes and her head fell forward a little.

Peggy crept over to the table by the window and opened the book. The first page was taken up by a title written in a neat and careful style: 'The Diary of William Shelton Trafford, gentmn.', it read, and underneath, 'October 1849 to ...' There was no closing date.

Peggy turned the page to the first entry and, to her delight, immediately saw the name Adam. Adam, but Adam who? And what did he mean in the story of the Traffords? He meant a lot to William Shelton Trafford, it was obvious, because every entry referred to him, usually as 'my friend Adam'.

She read slowly, for the handwriting of the diary was not as carefully formed as the title. But she read slowly because the diary was filled with details of wildlife, of the pleasures of nature that

William and his friend Adam discovered on the estate. 'On the estate,' she realized, was on what she knew as Adam's Common. She knew it from the atmosphere the diary created. She thought she even recognized the old oak tree she had found in the middle of the wood. It was Adam's Common, she knew, that William Trafford and this Adam were discovering together in the old yellow pages.

She had not yet come to the end of the diary when she heard Miss Trafford speak.

'You see,' she said. 'There was an Adam after all. Have you come to the end of it?'

'No,' said Peggy.

'Ring the bell for tea, and then you can take it home to read. That's if you promise to return it safe and sound.'

'I promise,' said Peggy.

She took the diary home and retreated to her bedroom with it. She felt that it was important to be alone when she read it, for a diary, even of someone long since dead, was a private thing.

Here and there in the diary to explain plants or fruits William and Adam had observed, there were delicate pencil drawings – not many, but they brightened the pages when they came.

The entries in the diary seemed to be made every day, though they weren't all dated. Once or twice the entry said simply 'No Adam', but the following entry would read, 'Adam came', or 'My friend came'.

Slowly, she worked her way through the book until she came to 18th December 1849. By now she felt she knew both Adam and William well. She shared their excitement at the discovery of a badger sett. She wondered if it was still to be found on the common.

On 19th December the entry read, 'No Adam'.

On 20th December again, 'No Adam'.

On 21st December it read, 'Still no Adam. It has been snowing. Perhaps that is why he hasn't come, the weather is so bad'.

On 22nd December, 'I went to the wall to see where Adam climbs over and waited. He did not come. On my way back Cousins the keeper saw me and told me it was dangerous there at night. He said there had been trouble with a poacher there two nights since. Cousins said he gave him more than he bargained for'.

On 23rd December the entry read, 'No Adam. I shall go into town to find him'.

On 24th December there were three words, 'I found him'. The words were scrawled across the page as if the writer had lost control of his pen.

'I found him. I found him.' The words echoed in Peggy's mind, and she wondered at their meaning.

There were no further entries. 'I found him' was the last in the little book. There were three blank pages left. So the diary, begun in October, had ended on Christmas Eve with the words 'I found him'.

Peggy's mood had changed. She had shared the pleasure of discovery with William and Adam; now she was strangely disturbed and anxious.

She went to bed telling herself, 'At any rate, I have found Adam. I have found him, too.'

TWENTY

Peggy Donovan turned away from the house. The dying sun struck redly from the fragments of glass in the windows and once again seemed to show the house aflame.

She had not meant to come out again to see it at night, for she did not like the thought of bats circling about the ruins. She tried to tell herself that the fear was foolish; bats were soft gentle creatures of the night and could do her no harm.

It was later than she had realized. The moon had not yet risen, and when she reached the wood, the darkness was intense. She could not understand why she had failed to notice how quickly time had passed. And it was cold, with a chill that belonged to winter, not to early summer. And the trees were bare; and, under her feet, the grass had a hard frosty feel. She looked down and saw there was a light sprinkling of snow at her feet.

As her eyes became accustomed to the dark and she looked around her, she could not tell where she was. She had thought all the paths of the common were familiar to her, but this one was not. She wondered where she had missed her way and thought she ought to retrace her steps until she got back to the path she knew, the one that led across the common back to home. But when she turned she became more confused. Whichever way she looked she seemed to face the same way, along the strange path, under bare branches. This was not the wild woodland she knew and loved. It was still the common, but it had a hostile feel to it, so that as she walked on she was afraid of what she might find in front of her.

She thought she could hear movement beside her, keeping pace with her along the path. Perhaps it's a fox, she thought, and stopped to look through the trees. She saw a shadowy figure flit from one tree to another, not a fox, but a human shape, then another, grey and furtive. She opened her mouth to call to them but no sound came. She walked on, conscious that her feet were making no sound, unlike the steps she could hear about her.

Then she heard a soft whistling, coming from in front, a light gay tune, half familiar to her in that it had echoes of folk songs she had heard back home. She stopped in her tracks and listened. The sound of the whistling came nearer and she waited to see who else was walking the common at this hour. From between the trees there stepped a boy, with black tousled hair, a thin face, large eyes, a mouth pursed to his whistling; he wore a long heavy jacket, too big for him at the shoulders and too long at the sleeves. His trousers were roughly shortened and ragged at the cuffs. And, in spite of the cold (Peggy felt it sharply and shivered), he was barefooted.

He did not seem to mind or feel the cold, for his soft whistle was cheerful and light-hearted, and he moved into the wood, toward Peggy, with firm step.

The sound of the other footsteps had died, and

Peggy thought she must have imagined the presence of others in the wood besides the boy; yet she had a feeling that they were still there, watching and waiting, and that, in their watching, they held danger for the boy.

He came on, unaware of Peggy or of the danger she could sense. At one point he stopped and bent down to the foot of a tree to search among the leaves, as if he had seen something of interest.

Then Peggy called out to him and this time her voice rose in a shrill cry, for she had seen two, three men, clad in dark clothes, one carrying a gun, moving stealthily forward.

The boy looked round at the cry and from above him an owl, which had screeched its warning, flew into the night.

'Got yer,' yelled a man, and the boy turned and ran, ran toward where Peggy, helpless, stood.

'Stop!' yelled the man with the gun and, before the word had died in the air, raised the gun and fired it at the boy. Peggy saw the boy stagger and turn his face toward her. His eyes were puzzled, his whistling had stopped and his lips tightened in a grimace of pain.

Peggy, deafened from the sound of the gunshot, went toward him, but he passed her in a halting uneven run, falling once and picking himself up, falling again and then crawling a yard or so, then lying still.

'That'll larn ye,' said the man with the gun; he called to his companions and they disappeared into the wood, indifferent to the figure lying under the trees.

Peggy, horrified at what she had seen and at her helplessness, stood looking down at the boy. She put out a hand to him, but as she did, he raised himself and with painful effort dragged himself farther. She could see blood on the ground where he had fallen, and a jagged trail of it in the snow, following him.

'Please!' she said. 'Let me help.' The boy might have heard, for he looked round and smiled, it seemed to her, before getting to his feet and moving from tree trunk to tree trunk. So, slowly he reached the edge of the wood and came to a high brick wall.

There were no walls round the common, so where could she be? She watched the boy reach for the top of the wall, saw his hands grip the coping stone, saw his fingers slip, saw the determination in his lips as he reached again, caught a firmer hold, and heaved himself up. She watched as he paused astride the wall to look back at her, or beyond her, before he dropped out of sight to the other side.

She called out, anxious to help, wanting to understand, but understanding nothing of what she had seen.

'Please!' she called again, and didn't know whom she was appealing to, or why.

She shivered, and wondered why, if it was winter, she was clad in summer clothes. Then she knew that the cold came from within her. The weather itself was mild, the air fragrant with the scents of the woodland. The trees were in leaf, there was no frost, the undergrowth was lush.

She was standing at the edge of the common. There was no wall, just a path, a low hedgerow and, beyond that, the Parade, noisy with the evening traffic, the roaring of car engines, the grating change of gears as trucks lumbered up the hill.

Peggy stepped back into the trees and looked

125

about her. There was no wall, there were no shadowy figures patrolling the common, there was no whistling boy, and there was no blood spattering the ground. But an owl in the trees above screeched as it hunted, and Peggy, disturbed and frightened at what she had seen, turned for home.

TWENTY-ONE

William Shelton Trafford put the documents in the deed box in the chest. He ought to deposit them with Lyons, Mather, and Lyons, the family lawyers. He must see to that some day.

He glanced around the library, of all the rooms in the house the one he used most. It had meant so much to him in the past. It was from here that he had watched the wood for . . . He suppressed the thoughts that came to him, or tried to. But he could never entirely drive them from his mind. As he looked around the shelves, he thought of the diary he had kept so many years before, when he was a boy of fourteen, in those times he chose now to forget. What had happened to it? he wondered. He searched half-heartedly on the shelves for it. He did not really want to find it, for it revived a painful and terrible memory.

What had happened to it? Perhaps it had gone to his cousin Humphrey when his parents died. He had been indifferent to the family heirlooms then. 'Let them go to Humphrey,' he had said. 'I want nothing of my family. I want no part of them.'

It had been impossible to forgive them. He had tried to make amends for the crime they had condoned, but what could he do for Adam?

127

There it was. The name was out. He tried to prevent the memory from flooding back, but there was no escaping it.

William Shelton Trafford went to the library window and looked across the garden and rockery (now sadly neglected) to the meadow and beyond to the woodlands. He still, knowing it to be nonsense, had a faint hope that he would see a shadow there under the trees, recognize the friend of his boyhood, and go to meet Adam, as he had done those many years ago.

He peered out. There was indeed a shadow there – an illusion again, as always nowadays – but somehow more substantial than that. It was the girl again, the tall fair-haired girl with the strange costume. He had seen her often coming out of the woods and crossing the meadow. He had seen her in the past and he saw her now and she did not seem to change. He had tried to attract her attention in the old days and had failed. She had sometimes been aware of him, he had thought, but when he had tried to speak to her, she had not understood.

As he watched her, he felt certain she had news of Adam. But no – that was out of the question. This girl was not of Adam's time. He did not know to what time she belonged, but it was not the dead past.

She crossed the meadow, hesitated at the ditch and then scrambled up. For a moment he had the illusion that it was Adam himself coming once again to summon him to join him in the woods.

Memory of his friend came thrusting back – hurtful memory – but there was no escape. He felt again the bitter disappointment of those days when Adam failed to arrive, felt the unease when Cousins had told him of the poacher, felt the guilt that seemed to hang about for days. And he remembered – remembered so vividly – how in defiance of his parents, he had walked into the town, gone to the squalid quarter by the river, and enquired for Adam.

'Adam?' The people he questioned had shaken their heads, had looked with curiosity at this boy from the wealthy sector of the town who ventured into their warren.

He had felt fear, recalling his first unpleasant experience there, but concern for Adam outweighed his terror, and thrusting through the crowds, he had continued his quest.

'Adam?' He did not know his friend's second name. It had not mattered.

'Adam?'

They had not wanted to speak to him. They were suspicious of him, resentful. He knew how they hated him, these people, with his warm clothes and his careful speech, his clear skin, and his easy manners.

He was not easy, for he remembered that time when he had fainted in the fetid air and had been robbed of his clothes. The air was not close and heavy now. It was cold, and the people huddled in their doorways against the biting December wind.

'Adam?' he had asked and then he had recognized a wispy-haired woman watching him from an alleyway. He had rushed to her, and though she had tried to evade him, he had grasped hold of her. He had taken her thin, bony arm in his strong hand. It was Ma Thackrey. He remembered her well.

'Adam,' he had said. 'You know him. Adam.'

'Adam,' she croaked. 'I know him. Or I did. They killed him, di'n't they?' She spat and her spittle only just missed William's shoe.

'They killed 'im.'

He stared at her and his grip tightened, so that she looked afraid.

'Who killed him?' William's mouth uttered the question, though his mind could not accept it. 'Killed him? Who?'

'They did.' She gestured vaguely over her shoulder. 'Who d'yer think?' She snatched her arm away. 'He never did no one any harm. Not Adam.' She moved off.

William seized her arm again.

'Who? I said. Who?'

'Them up there. The keepers on the estate. The Traffords and their keepers, that's who.'

'Let go of me,' she said when his grip tightened. But he could not let her go. She was his only connection with his friend.

'I don't understand,' he said helplessly.

The woman looked at him, almost in sympathy. 'I'll show thee,' she said.

He had followed her away from the riverbank to a quiet graveyard by a small church. She had led him to a freshly dug, unmarked grave. 'There he is,' she had said. 'Adam. There he is.'

He had let her go at that and stood, shivering, unable to speak, unable to move. He had found Adam.

TWENTY-TWO

Peggy opened the diary again. 'William Shelton Trafford, gentmn.', she read. What sort of boy was he? She thought she knew. She had seen him, had almost been able to talk to him.

She had seen Adam too, she had no doubt. The boy with the wide eyes, the gentle mouth, the ragged clothes, who had left his trail of blood in the snow – that was Adam.

The experience in the wood had frightened her, but she was still determined to go back to the house. There she had met the boy William Trafford. He had known Adam. He would have the key to Adam's Common. She would go to find him, to meet him, to challenge him to tell her the answer.

She slept soundly. The terror of the scene in the woods did not haunt her dreams. More peaceful pictures rested in her mind, of two boys observing a badger, of their walks through the woodland, of their friendship for each other.

She woke with a feeling of warm understanding. She saw the diary open by her bed, the diary that told of William Trafford and Adam.

It was early and she thought she would have time before school to visit the house again, if she was quick with her breakfast.

131

'Really, Peggy,' said her mother. 'What's got into you? Take your time. What's the hurry?'

'I want to go to the house before school.'

'The house?'

'Trafford Court. The house I drew.'

'Well, don't spend too long there. I know how time goes by when you're sketching.'

'I'm not going to draw,' said Peggy. 'Just to look.'

And to explore, she admitted to herself.

'I won't be here when you get back from school,' said her mother. 'I'll leave you something to eat. It's the meeting tonight, remember, when the fate of the common will be decided. The committee's getting together before that, to prepare our statements.'

Peggy had forgotten how little time was left to save the common.

'You'll join me at the meeting, Peggy?'

'I'll be there.'

'What shall I tell Steven? He'll come for you on his way to school.'

'Tell him where I've gone. But I'll see him at school. Bye, Mum.'

She hurried across the common. It was almost empty of people at this time of day. A light morning mist clung to the bushes.

Today the house had changed its mood again. She had seen it before as friendly, sorrowful, restful, threatening. It was none of these things now; it was challenging, as if to say, 'I am here, waiting for you to find my secret.'

She crossed the meadow, climbed up from the ditch to the garden rockery and walked up to the door of the house without hesitation, suppressing the fears that had niggled at her before. It was as if she was paying a formal visit upon the people of the house, responding to an invitation to call.

Indeed, when she got to the door, she knocked without thinking and paused, waiting for someone to come to open to her.

The sound of her fist on the door echoed within the house and the door swung slightly with her pressure. She pushed it open further. It groaned as she opened it wide. She stood on the threshold.

William Shelton Trafford could not free his mind of the thought of Adam. Whenever he looked out on to the garden and to the woodland beyond, he saw, in his mind's eye, the boy he had grown to love.

He looked out now from his library. There was no Adam there, no Adam. He closed his eyes in sadness at his thoughts. No Adam, but, as he opened his eyes again, he saw the girl, the girl who, somehow, was linked in his mind with Adam. He felt she too had known Adam, had seen them together.

She would understand. She would know what friendship meant; it would be good to know her, to invite her into the house, to encourage her to wander over Adam's Common. The common was hers; it belonged to her and every child. It was there for her to enjoy, as Adam had enjoyed it.

She would understand.

As she looked, he realized she had come for a purpose. It must be to look for him. He was certain she was as anxious to speak to him as he was to speak to her.

He went to the door and opened it for her. He waited for her to speak.

She looked at him, and through him.

She looks at me and sees nothing, he thought with sharp surprise. He opened his mouth and spoke softly, so as not to startle her.

She heard, it seemed, for she turned her head in his direction.

'Adam,' he whispered. 'Do you know him?'

'Adam,' he said again, more loudly now. 'They killed him, you know. I tried to make amends.'

She does not hear me, he thought, and in desperation tried to reach out to take her by the arm, but she seemed anxious and turned away, back to the garden.

Peggy stood at the door, looking in at the debris. It was quiet within. There was no wind to send leaves scuttering to her feet, no stirring of small creatures. There was silence, total and enclosing. The silence of time, she said to herself. The years have left this silence here, a whole and secret silence.

I dare not break it, she told herself. It belongs to itself not to me.

A soft sound came to her, more within her mind than from outside. She turned her head, wondering what it was that had caught her attention.

I shall be late for school, she thought, and turned to go, reluctantly, for she felt she was on the verge of breaking through a barrier.

'Adam,' she said aloud, for at that moment she could think of nothing else.

'Adam,' she heard and wondered how, in the garden, an echo could form.

She turned to look back at the house, school forgotten, and at that moment felt a touch upon her hand, a gentle touch, encouraging her, leading her back to the house.

She saw nothing, but the soft sensation on her hand was there. She was no longer hesitant. The house would not resent her intrusion. She was welcome.

'You saw him?' A voice came to her. 'You knew him too? Adam?'

A man was standing beside her.

He smiled.

'I did not startle you, I hope.'

She tried to answer but could not. You did surprise me, she said to herself, coming as you did out of nowhere.

His hand upon her arm was gentle but firm.

'You'll come with me?' he said. 'There's something I want you to see.'

She went with him, helpless to resist that light compelling touch. She glanced at him out of the corner of her eye. His clothes were of an unusual cut, but she had seen them before, in that stiff, formal portrait of Miss Trafford's ancestor.

Then she knew. There was about him, the way he moved noiselessly through the grass, his voice so soft as to be hardly more than a stirring of the air, there was about him nothing that was substantial, though his presence was real. His fingers touched her, but she felt no flesh; she heard his voice, without sound; she saw him, but not, somehow, with her eyes. He was there within her, drawing her mind to his.

What did he want of her?

It has to do with Adam, it must be, she heard herself say, with the common that belonged to Adam. That is all that matters.

Without fear she went with him.

'I will show you,' she heard. 'They killed him.

135

Did you know? They killed Adam. I tried to make amends but I could not bring him back.'

She felt a desperate sadness invade her.

She allowed herself to be led into the house. She was astonished. There were no cobwebs, no charred timbers, no fluttering bats. Light shone from candles burning in a shimmering chandelier; broad stairs led from the hall to the upstairs rooms; the walls were lined with the portraits of lordly figures.

They passed along a corridor into a book-lined room, a working, busy room, with a large desk on one side, with papers spread upon it, and beside it a metal trunk.

She was led to the window. It looked out to the garden. She could see the rock where she had sat to draw the house.

'I saw you,' she heard. 'From here. You were drawing. I came to help you, I think. It was so long ago I don't remember.'

She remembered. It was only the other day.

She stood at the window, wondering what she was doing here, knowing there were questions to ask, but unsure of what they were.

'He shot him. Cousins, the keeper, did it, I'm sure. They sent him away afterward. They would tell me nothing, but I knew. I knew what had happened.'

The touch of his hand seemed to tighten.

'I hated them. I shouldn't, I suppose, but I had had a friend, and he was gone.'

Peggy looked around at the room. It was a peaceful room, she felt, a welcoming room. She would have liked to browse among the leather-bound books on the shelves, but her attention was held by the voice.

'William Shelton Trafford. I came into the estate when my parents were killed. An accident – on the very railway he helped to build. I thought I could make amends at last. But how could I? Adam was dead. I could not trace his family.'

Time had ceased to have meaning for Peggy. She wanted to tell William Trafford she understood. She could not speak, but he seemed to know what she wanted to say. He had turned away from her and she saw his silhouette at the window.

'It was an offence to me, the Trafford money. I had a hospital built on what used to be Riverbank. A hospital – that wasn't enough. It could not make Adam whole again. Then I thought of his love of nature, the joy he got from the creatures of the earth, the plants of meadow and woodland. So all this, between here and the town, I transferred to the Borough. I had the walls destroyed. Welcomed the children of Traverton. Made it possible for them to come and go as they please – the Adams and the Zackys, and the Thackrey boys.' (She wondered who he was talking about.) 'I opened it to them all – to wander over at will, without let or hindrance, for ever more. And' – he turned back to her – 'you will understand,' he said, 'as a mark of my friendship it was to be known as Adam's Common.'

He seemed to disappear from sight and Peggy thought she was alone again, but a sigh came to her and she felt a touch upon her hand again.

'I must show you,' the voice came, 'my copy of the deed of transfer, my tribute to his memory, my friend, Adam. I tried to make amends, make amends.'

She could not bear the sadness in his voice and

wanted to beg him to stop. 'You did make amends,' she wanted to say. 'The children of Traverton know it. They love Adam's Common, even if they do not know of Adam.'

She closed her eyes, trying to concentrate, to convey to William Trafford her understanding of him.

He has gone, she said to herself, he has gone. She opened her eyes and knew she was alone. The whispers she could hear were those of the wind sighing through the broken walls. She was alone, in a room cluttered with debris. There were no shelves burdened with leather-bound volumes; there was no desk strewn with papers; there was no metal chest.

'I must show you my copy of the deed of transfer.' Her heart leaped as she remembered what he had said. But where?

'Come back, come back,' she called, but her voice carried emptily through the ruins, and there was no reply.

She looked around her, at the rubble heaped about. No trace of books, no desk, no metal chest.

There was.

From beneath the sodden plaster, the jumbled stone, there was a thin gleam of metal, the corner of a box, she thought, a metal box or chest.

She suddenly came to her senses. I have come here for a purpose, she told herself. I was brought here for a purpose. I know that it is here, all that is needed to save the common. I only have to look. I knew all along. Adam's name was the key.

I'm late for school, she said. I must go now and come back later. There isn't time, she argued with herself. The meeting is this evening. If there's anything to be found, it must be found now.

She tried to reach over the clutter of rubble toward the jutting corner of the box but her footing was treacherous and, as she bent forward, she slipped and fell through a gaping hole, with a scatter of dust.

At first she thought she had fallen into a cellar, but realized it was only into the shallow foundations of the house. She could easily scramble back into the room above. Or could if she could overcome the pain.

It was her left ankle that hurt. She put her hand to it and felt it cautiously. She tried to move her foot, but a sharp, agonizing pang spread up her leg and she thought she was going to faint.

TWENTY-THREE

Steven Walsh was concerned. Peggy Donovan had not appeared at school. He could not think what had happened to her. When he had called for her in the morning, Mrs Donovan had told him Peggy would see him at school.

'She's gone to see that old house, Trafford Court, for some reason best known to herself,' Peggy's mother had said.

Steven knew of Trafford Court. It had stood empty for years and then, a year or two since, had burned down. It was not the sort of place he would be tempted to visit. It was rumoured to be haunted – and that was why it had been unoccupied for so long, people said. It wasn't the stories of ghosts that kept him away, he told himself. He wasn't afraid of ghosts – he didn't believe in them anyway.

It was just not his sort of place and he could not understand what it was about it that made it so interesting to Peggy.

'Have you seen Peggy?' he asked Marion Harper at lunch.

She looked at Steven. 'Peggy Donovan?' She pouted and shrugged her shoulders. 'No, I haven't.' She was turning away when she saw Steven's worry was genuine.

'Is she missing or something?' she asked.

'I don't know. I expected her to come to school. Her mother said she was coming.'

Marion looked pityingly at him. 'Then I expect she'll turn up this afternoon. It's a nice day. Perhaps she thought it would be nicer out of school than in.'

'She's not like that,' said Steven.

'Maybe not,' said Marion. 'But it's nothing to get bothered about.'

Steven was bothered, and when Peggy did not appear in the afternoon for her favourite subject, art, he was sure there was something wrong.

'Well?' said Marion at the end of the afternoon. 'She didn't come then?'

Steven shook his head. 'I wonder what's happened to her?' he said.

'Nothing. You're getting all worked up over nothing,' Marion said. 'You wouldn't be so anxious if I missed a day, would you?'

Steven looked at her in surprise. 'Well, nothing would happen to you,' he said.

'Oh, and what can have happened to Peggy Donovan, then, that couldn't happen to me?'

'It's not that,' said Steven, fumbling for an explanation. 'She's been strange recently.'

'So you've noticed,' said Marion, then, when she again saw Steven's worried expression, she added, 'I was only joking.'

She linked her arm through Steven's.

'Come on,' she said. 'We'd better go and see if she's at home. I expect she'll be sitting there gorging herself on chocolate cake or something.'

Steven was glad of Marion's company, especially when there was no reply at the Donovans'.

'I must go and look for her,' he said.

'Where?'

'Trafford Court,' he said. 'That's where she was going, her mother said.'

'I'll come with you,' said Marion. 'I'll have tea first and come back for you.'

Steven did not tell his mother of his concern for Peggy. In any case she was in a hurry to get away to the demonstration and the meeting about the common.

When Marion arrived, they set off together across the common.

'Trafford Court's haunted, you know,' said Marion.

'Nonsense,' said Steven, but when they came to the barbed wire and the notice saying NO ENTRY – STRICTLY PRIVATE, he wondered if they should go on.

'I don't like this,' said Marion, but, when Steven turned to her, he saw she was complaining of the thorns and brambles, not of the sinister forces that Steven began to imagine surrounding them.

He forced his way through nevertheless, and Marion followed until they came to the edge of the woodland and saw, in front of them, the gaunt ruins of the house.

'It looks spooky,' said Marion.

'We can't turn back now,' said Steven, uneasily aware that he wanted to.

'I didn't mean we should turn back,' said Marion impatiently. 'I only said it looks spooky. I didn't say it was.'

There was an atmosphere about the place – the meadow with its tall weeds, the distant prospect of the house with its tumbled walls, the loneliness – that made Steven pause. He was not

142

sure he wanted to go on. Perhaps he had been mistaken. Perhaps this was not the house Peggy had gone to see.

'Well?' said Marion, stepping across the meadow toward the house, 'Are you coming?'

TWENTY-FOUR

I will not faint, Peggy told herself, the pain is not so bad. But it was bad; whenever she put her weight on her left foot, it caused her to cry out with agony.

She felt ashamed of herself for the cries, but she could not help it. Her shout had echoed about the ruins, so that she had hoped it would bring William Trafford to her aid. Of course he can't help, she told herself. He's not really here.

He is, she said, for he spoke to me, he touched me, and he was about to show me . . .

She forgot the pain in her ankle as she remembered why she was here in the ruined house, why William Trafford had spoken to her. She could see the metal box from where she was, and she thought, I can heave myself out of here and get to it.

It was almost within reach, but when she stretched out her arm to it, she dislodged rubble and plaster. A flurry of dust rose and made her sneeze so violently that she moved her leg and was aware again of the pain in her ankle.

She felt a sudden panic. She was here, alone, injured, in a house that no one but she ever visited. And she was here within reach of the answer to the mystery of Adam's Common. She was here, helpless, while only a mile or so away in a few hours the fate of the common would be sealed.

She looked for her wrist watch, but in her fall, the strap had broken and the watch had gone. She bent down to feel at her feet, but it was no use. All she could feel was rubbish, charred wood that crumbled to dust at her touch. She was ankle deep in the stuff.

She began to feel sorry for herself; but that would do no good, she reminded herself, nor would it help to save the common.

She had to move, whatever the pain, had to struggle to the chest to find what was within it. She tried to remember what William Trafford had said, 'the deed of transfer', and he had seemed to point then at the metal chest beside his desk.

She must get out of this hole. She put her elbows up on the floor and heaved. The boards were rotten, what was left of them, but she managed to drag herself up, out of the foundations, though the effort exhausted her.

She was hungry, she realized, and parched with thirst, because of the dust that swirled about her and which she took in with every breath. It must be late; her stomach told her it was long past lunch time; it must already be teatime. She thought of the muffins she had promised herself. And tea! A cup of tea! She did not often drink tea, but now she longed for a cup.

It was no use longing or wishing or feeling hungry. She had to do something to help herself. There was no one else at hand, not even William Trafford. She wondered if he would come if she called.

145

'Mr Trafford,' she called, but not too loudly. If he were there, he would hear her.

The sound died in a whisper about the fallen rafters.

She sat and examined her ankle. It was swollen and puffy, but the pain was less now. If she moved carefully, it would not hurt her much. She took off her shoe and moved her toes. She did not think she had broken any bones, but her ankle was too sore to bear her weight.

It will have to bear my weight, Peggy said to herself, for I have to do so much and there is so little time. She got slowly to her feet and tested her ankle for a second. But it was too much; the pain that shot through her was almost unbearable.

She sat down again and looked about her for something to use as a crutch to help her stand. There were pieces of timber, but all were too large and all too fragile from the fire to be of much use.

All around, unsorted debris from the fire cluttered the room. It seemed that no one could have ventured in here since the disaster struck. For whatever reason, the room seemed to be as it had been when the fire exhausted itself, rubble heaped together, and hiding all but a corner of the metal chest.

She inched herself over to it, through the dust, pushing aside the jagged wreckage in her way. She pushed at the debris piled on top of the chest and it shifted, but with it more debris fell. She heard a rumble as if the walls were moving, settling, or she thought fancifully, as if they were grumbling at her intrusion.

'It's all right,' she said aloud, as if to reassure the house she meant no harm. She was getting

146

light-headed from hunger and pain and the strange events of the day.

She reached out again to the metal chest and felt it under the rubble. The touch encouraged her, and she felt around the box for something to get hold of to drag it from under its layer of dust and wreckage.

She found a hasp and began to tug at the chest. It resisted, but then, suddenly, yielded, and as it did timber, plaster, and stone cascaded about her in a storm of dust.

TWENTY-FIVE

'I heard something,' said Steven Walsh, and hesitated.

Marion Harper turned to look at him, put her hands on her hips and shook her head.

'I do believe you're scared,' she said.

'I heard something,' Steven repeated.

'Ghosts, I suppose,' said Marion scornfully.

'Didn't you hear anything?' he asked. 'Listen. Can't you hear?'

They stopped together, surrounded by giant thistles and great dandelions. A puff of wind sent seedlets from the flowers floating past.

They were silent, waiting for something.

'There's nothing,' said Marion and moved to go on.

'Wait,' said Steven, and put his hand on her arm. 'There.'

There was a faint rumble, like distant thunder.

'What do you think it was?' he asked.

Marion shrugged her shoulders. 'Are we looking for Peggy, or aren't we?' she said. 'If we're not, we might as well go back.'

Steven almost agreed. He did not like the place. The house at the end of the meadow stood dark against the sky, its outlines broken, a skeleton with its limbs awry. To Steven there was nothing picturesque or romantic in its shape. He could believe its fallen rooms were peopled with phantoms, cruel, malevolent spirits. He was not usually given to flights of imagination, but now he recoiled from the place and wanted to flee from it.

'Shall we give up and go back?' Marion said in a matter-of-fact way.

'No,' said Steven. 'We've not searched properly. Peggy may be here.'

'Call her then.'

Together they stood on the edge of the meadow and called, 'Peggy! Peggy!'

There was no answer.

'Peggy! Peggy!' they called again.

A large black bird, a rook, rose from among the ruins and flew into the trees behind the house.

'Did you hear anything?' said Steven.

'I'm not sure,' Marion answered.

Steven climbed up from the ditch and, slowly, uncertainly, approached the house.

TWENTY-SIX

Peggy shook herself free of dust thinking: This time I really have hurt myself. The chest lay on top of her, and her leg, the one with the injured ankle, was bent under her. I've broken something now, she thought. She tried to move, but the weight on her was too great.

She thought she must have fainted and had been unconscious for some time, but she could not tell. She was empty with hunger and her mouth and throat were burning with thirst. She tried to call out but had not strength enough to utter more than a whimper, and then a hoarse, almost soundless croak.

She shifted her shoulder and the chest moved. If she wriggled to her right she thought she could perhaps slip from under it and from most of the weight. She dragged herself back a little and felt the chest move again and leave her free, or almost. There was still a weight across her legs.

She rested a moment to recover her strength, for her efforts to free herself had exhausted her. Then slowly, she bent over to see what was holding her legs down. It was a jagged beam leaning against her. Blood had dried just below her knee; it must have flowed freely before it clotted, she thought.

She reached down, and taking hold of the wood, raised it from her legs. It was heavy and awkward but she found she could move it aside. It lay where she pushed it, raising a cloud of dust.

Now that she was free of the weight, the pain in her leg did not seem so bad. She was able to straighten it; she examined the wound at her knee and saw there was a raw, deep cut. The sight of it made her feel faint again.

It's no good passing out, she told herself. I've got to get out of here. But first, she remembered, I have to find what I came for.

What did I come for? she wondered, and could not clear her mind. And where am I? she asked herself. There were moments when she was not even sure of that.

'Pull yourself together,' she said. 'I'm starving,' she answered herself, 'faint with hunger. Then find a way,' she said. 'Work it out for yourself. Think. Be calm.' She said the last words aloud, in a painful hoarse voice.

Her thoughts suddenly turned to her mother, and she remembered then the importance of the day for them all. Unless, she thought with fright, that day has passed. She had been unconscious, she realized, but did not know if it was for mere seconds, or much, much longer.

Her mind was wandering and she knew she must not let it drift. She must concentrate hard if she was to escape. But it was very hard to think clearly with the gnawing ache in her stomach. 'I shall talk to myself,' she said, 'even if it does hurt my throat. I shall keep myself awake by describing things to myself.' And she looked around her and began.

'There's a dark corner at the back,' she said

hoarsely. 'I don't know what's there except rubbish. There's a window over in the wall, I think, behind that pile of debris. I can't see it, but it must be there, because there's daylight creeping in. And there's a metal chest.'

A metal chest. It was lying beside her. 'It's important to open it,' she said aloud. 'Open it. Open it,' she kept repeating to herself, gazing dreamily at the chest and wondering what it was all about.

'Open it,' she said and then, in surprise, added, 'It is open.'

The surprise woke her fully and she realized she had been dozing, that she had imagined she had been talking, or listening to someone else talking.

'Lift the lid,' she heard, and she lifted the lid, certain that within the chest she would find what she was seeking. The lid creaked and resisted, rust on the hinges preventing it from opening wide. She pushed it upward and saw with disappointment that, though the chest itself seemed intact, fire had reached inside somehow and had left nothing, it seemed, but black cinders of paper, falling to ashes as she fingered them.

There was something though, beneath the ashes – a separate inner compartment, or another box, also of metal. She wiped the ashes from it and examined it. It was a box, made of steel, and barely defaced by the heat that had destroyed so much else.

By now the dreaminess that had clouded her eyes before had gone. She was intent upon the box, determined to probe its secrets, but the box was secured with a padlock in a hasp that was welded to the box. She pulled at the padlock but it held firm.

'The key,' she said aloud. 'The key. It must be here.' She searched in the chest among the black fluttering paper ashes. It could be there, she thought. I have been lucky so far, she said to herself, forgetting the aches and pains, the cuts and bruises, lucky to find the chest, and lucky to find the box. And as she scrabbled about with her fingers, fortune smiled on her again, and she felt a key. She took hold of it, fitted it to the lock and turned it. It stuck, as if reluctant to reveal its secrets, then moved, yielding. Peggy threw open the lid and looked inside.

TWENTY-SEVEN

Peggy put her hand into the box and withdrew a scroll, a roll of parchment, tied with a ribbon of faded blue and gold. Attached to the ribbon was a large red seal stamped with a shield of arms. She carefully untied the ribbon and unrolled the parchment. The lettering on it was elaborately penned in black, and at the top, two shields of arms were drawn in heraldic colours, one of the town, and the other, the shield of arms she had seen on the house, which she knew to be those of the Trafford family.

She followed the writing on the manuscript slowly, for the unfamiliarity of the script made it difficult to read, but the purpose was clear, and as she read, she became aware she had found the key she had been seeking, that vital piece of hard legal evidence to save Adam's Common.

Her eyes burned with tears of joy, and with the pain of concentration. 'To transfer to the Borough of Traverton, for the leisure of its citizens, and to provide for the children of the Borough, an open space preserved as nature intended it, to be enjoyed in perpetuity by those same children, free of any let or hindrance ... not to be built upon in any way ... that portion of land marked in red on the plan adjoined, this said land to be

154

known in future as Adam's Common . . .'

She did not need to read further, she did not need to see the plan; she had found the answer. She could not prevent herself calling out, 'Yippee! I've found it! Yippee!' The words came out as a raucous croak.

'Did you hear something?' said Steven, pausing by a large rock in the garden.

'Yes,' said Marion. 'A rook cawing, that's all.'

'No, it wasn't,' said Steven. 'It was something else.'

They drew near the house and walked along the walls, trying to peer through the gaps into the dark space within.

The sound came again, but louder, though still hoarse and unearthly.

'What was that?' said Steven, stopping in his tracks.

'It sounded like yippee to me,' said Marion.

'Peggy?' said Steven. Then he called, 'Peggy!'

'It came from over there,' said Marion, and they ran together to a place where broken mullion showed a window, looking from the house to the garden.

'Peggy!' called Marion. 'Are you there?'

'I've found it,' came the answer. 'I've found it!'

Steven tried to see into the room from which the voice came, but there was a pile of debris barring his way. He scrambled up and began to push at the rubble.

'Hey! Watch out,' called Peggy in protest. 'Not that way.'

'Be careful, Steven,' warned Marion. 'Are you all right, Peggy?'

'I've found it,' came the reply again.

155

'What have you found?' said Steven, looking around for a safer way into the room. He ran to the door and stumbled along over stone and brick and plaster. It was dark in the corners of the house, dark and forbidding, but he ignored his terrors.

'Where are you?' he called, and his voice carried up to where birds were nesting. Disturbed, they rose as a flock, wings beating noisily. Steven held his breath, then called again. 'Where are you?'

'Here,' croaked Peggy. 'Oh Steven, am I glad to see you!'

Marion peered over Steven's shoulder. 'Hi!' she said in her cheeriest voice. 'You do look a fright! What's that?' she added, as she saw Peggy holding up, out of the dust, a scroll of parchment.

'It's the evidence,' said Peggy. 'The evidence that's needed to save the common. What time is it?'

'Nearly seven o'clock,' said Steven, warily stepping over the debris toward Peggy.

'Oh heavens,' she said. 'The meeting starts at seven-thirty. Let's get out, please.' She tried to stand but yelped with pain.

'You're hurt,' exclaimed Steven.

'It's nothing,' said Peggy. 'Let's go.'

'Lean on me,' said Marion.

Peggy tried to put her foot down to walk, with Marion's support, but it was no use, for each movement she made brought tears to her eyes.

'Steven,' she said. 'Go for Walter Lyons. He's the one we need.'

'Why?' said Steven, looking with horror at the gash on Peggy's knee. 'It's a doctor you need, not a lawyer.'

'Walter Lyons,' she said firmly. 'Go on. Don't waste time.'

Steven looked at Marion for guidance.

'Do as she says,' said Marion. 'And be quick about it.'

He hastened away, and with Marion's help, Peggy managed to move slowly out of the house, to sit on the rock in the garden.

'You do look a mess,' said Marion. 'Let me have a look at your leg.'

Marion bent down to examine the wound and then looked up at Peggy. 'You'll live,' she said.

'Thank you,' said Peggy with heavy sarcasm.

Marion grinned, not at all put out. She seemed to have forgotten she had ever been unfriendly.

Peggy sat clutching the scroll and Marion sat beside her. There didn't seem to be any need for them to speak, until Peggy anxiously asked the time.

'Seven-fifteen,' said Marion.

'Oh, come on,' said Peggy. 'Come on. Where are they?'

TWENTY-EIGHT

Walter Lyons was unhappy. The Common Defence Committee had entrusted him with the responsibility of presenting their case to the public meeting. He had no hope he could persuade the council to give way, for he had failed to find any evidence to prove that the council was beyond its rights in handing the common to developers.

He was bound to let the committee down, he felt, bound to disappoint the campaign's supporters. If he had a shred of evidence, he could make a case, but he had nothing.

The committee had worked so hard, all of them, especially young Peggy Donovan with her posters and placards, that they deserved to win. Yet, they were going to lose. At the meeting in less than an hour's time, Councillor Brookes would sign the contract to ruin Adam's Common.

Adam's Common; his heart stirred at the thought of it, and sadly, he sat down to prepare his speech in its defence. It would have to be an appeal to emotion and tradition; he could do that well enough, but it would not carry much weight with the council.

Still . . . He put pen to paper.

A knock came at the door, an impatient rat-a-tat.

Annoyed at the interruption, he called, 'Come in.'

The door opened and a breathless, hot, and red-faced boy stood panting at the entrance. Walter recognized him as being from Town School, a friend of Peggy Donovan's.

'Please, sir,' the boy gasped. 'Please, sir.' He paused to take a deep breath, and Walter, puzzled, waited.

'It's Peggy,' the boy said at last. 'Peggy Donovan. She's hurt, but it's not that. She said to fetch you.' He stopped, again out of breath. 'She's found something. Something important, she says.'

'Where is she?'

'At Trafford Court. Her leg's bad.'

'You should have got an ambulance or gone for a doctor, or her mother,' said Walter.

'No, sir. Peggy said it must be you. You'd know what to do. Are you coming, sir?' He waited on the threshold expecting the lawyer to move at his bidding.

'I can't just drop everything,' said Walter.

'Please, sir,' said Steven. 'There's no time to lose. The meeting, you see.'

'The meeting! I know all about the meeting. I've a speech to get ready for it.'

'You must come, sir. Peggy said it's important for the meeting. It's got to be you. You'd know if it's the right evidence, she said.'

'Evidence? What evidence?'

'She's found something, an old document, at Trafford Court.'

Walter Lyons looked at the boy. It wasn't possible, surely, but suddenly he saw a glimmer of hope.

'Trafford Court, you say?'

'Yes.'

'Right. Let's go.' He ran out of the office to his car. 'Get in.'

They'll have to find someone else to make the case for the common, if I don't get back in time, he thought, as he drove with unaccustomed recklessness out of the town toward Trafford Court. There was an entrance to the estate, he knew, to the south, along winding country lanes past farmland that had once belonged to the Traffords.

'Hold tight,' he said to Steven as, horn blaring, he took corners at speed. 'Hold tight.'

He was exhilarated and as hopeful as he had been miserable before. There is a chance, he told himself, still a chance of saving the common.

'How badly is she hurt?' he asked the boy.

'She says it's nothing, but it looks nasty,' Steven replied. 'She must have been lying there a long time.'

'We'll get her to hospital,' said Walter.

If we don't land up there first, thought Steven, as they narrowly avoided a farm cart and swerved between two granite pillars, with only inches to spare.

TWENTY-NINE

Elizabeth Donovan approached the Town Hall with much less than her usual enthusiasm. She had seen how dispirited Walter Lyons had been at their committee meeting. Well, they had all done their best, and if they failed to save the common, it would not be for lack of trying.

As she climbed the steps to the meeting room, she looked for Peggy, half expecting to see her among the people assembling for the meeting. Perhaps it's as well she's not here, she thought; she'd be heartbroken at the likely outcome.

She looked for Walter Lyons, but there was no sign of him either. She supposed he was busy preparing his speech. Poor Walter! He would be heartbroken too.

'Well done, Mrs Donovan,' she heard a woman say, someone she had never seen before. 'We'll show them, won't we?' She was touched by the woman's faith and drew fresh courage from it.

A man in work clothes, as if he had come straight from the factory, came up to her and said, 'More power to your elbow, Mrs Donovan,' before he turned to go into the meeting.

I wish I could have done more, she said to herself and went into the council chamber. It was a large, dignified, semicircular room, with three high-backed chairs, rather like thrones, set on a dais at the far end of the room. In front of them was a large, solid table with several chairs placed at it. Tiers of seats rose around the chamber, and every one seemed to be occupied. As Elizabeth Donovan went in, she was greeted, to her surprise, by a burst of applause. A hand waved from the front row and she saw Mr Richards, the teacher from Peggy's school, sitting with other committee members. 'Here,' he called, 'we've saved you a seat.'

'Where's Walter?' she asked.

'I don't know,' said Mr Richards. 'If he doesn't come, you'll have to speak.'

'I can't do that,' protested Mrs Donovan. 'It's not my campaign.'

'You and your daughter have made it yours,' he replied. 'Perhaps without you we'd never have got started.'

The buzz in the room grew and then paused in expectation as a number of men came into the hall from behind the thrones, the mayor and the town clerk, and, looking jaunty and smug, Councillor Brookes, the chairman of the Planning Committee. Three clerks, with rolled plans under their arms, sat at the table and were joined by another man, a tall, smartly dressed, florid-faced man, with iron-grey hair.

'The chairman of the development company,' whispered Richards.

At the back of the hall, where people unable to find seats were standing, a commotion grew.

'Let me through,' a shrill voice called, and down the steps leading to the floor of the hall a wheelchair was carried.

'Good Lord,' said Richards. 'Old Miss

162

Trafford. Who would have thought it?'

The meeting began, in an ordered decorous way that would have pleased Walter Lyons, thought Elizabeth Donovan.

The mayor expressed his gratification that so many citizens were present to mark what was likely to prove a significant day in the history of the town. He seemed to have no expectation of opposition. He introduced (saying there was no need for introduction) Councillor Brookes, whose 'energy and enterprise have been largely responsible for this exciting development'.

There was no hint yet of dissent among the assembled people. No voice had been raised so far against the plan, no question asked. Councillor Brookes spoke, at length, mouthing orotund, pompous phrases with practised ease.

Elizabeth Donovan let her mind wander. She was worried at the prospect of having to speak. At home it would have been easy enough, but here she was among strangers. She wondered what she could say to counter this claptrap.

'Claptrap,' she repeated and was astonished to realize she had spoken aloud, in a moment when Councillor Brookes had paused to draw breath. 'Claptrap,' she repeated with more vigour, and the meeting broke into uproar, with a loud burst of applause, and a sudden instantaneous display of a forest of placards, appearing as if at a command, around the hall.

'Claptrap!' the cry was taken up from several quarters, and even above the hubbub, the piping voice of old Miss Trafford made itself heard. 'Claptrap,' it said. 'That's what it is, right enough.'

The mayor looked at a loss for words. He stood,

a small dumpy man in his mayoral robes, trying to impose his authority upon these unruly citizens. Things like this don't happen in my council chamber, he seemed to be saying, but he could not be heard for the pandemonium that had erupted.

Elizabeth Donovan was surprised at herself. She had not consciously interrupted Councillor Brookes, but once she had, she was determined to keep the initiative. If I have to speak, now's the time, she thought. She rose to her feet, shook her head with a gesture of defiance at the platform and raised her hand.

Silence fell.

THIRTY

Walter stared at Peggy Donovan. 'My goodness,' he said. 'You are in a state!'

'I've found it,' she answered, flourishing the scroll.

He ignored her. 'What on earth have you done to yourself? Your clothes, and good heavens, that leg! We must get you to a doctor straight away.'

'Look at that,' she said impatiently and thrust the scroll at him. 'It's evidence, the evidence you wanted, I'm sure.'

He took it from her, unrolled it, and with an expert eye read it, his eyes opening wide in amazement.

'By heavens!' he said. 'This is it. This is it!' he repeated in a shout of delight. He looked at his watch. 'Oh Lord, we'll be too late.'

'Come on, then,' said Peggy, stumbling to her feet and dragging at his arm.

'The doctor first,' he said.

'The meeting,' she replied.

'The doctor.'

'The meeting.'

Walter yielded. Peggy held on to Marion and hobbled to Walter's car, the sporty red car which, he had said, was out of keeping with his character.

His character has changed then, thought

Peggy, as he drove into town, changing gear like a rally driver, taking corners at speed, ignoring traffic lights and, with tyres shrieking, pulled up at the foot of the Town Hall steps.

'Come on,' he called. 'We've not a moment to lose.'

With Peggy supported between Marion and Steven, her feet hardly touching the ground, they mounted the steps. They could hear angry sounds coming from the council chamber. Two policemen, large placid figures, stood at the door. They turned to prevent the entry of the latecomers, but they recognized Walter and allowed them in.

For a moment they stood looking on the scene. Councillor Brookes was standing, red-faced and angry, shaking a fist at the assembly, then pointing a threatening finger at Peggy's mother, who, ignoring his protests, was addressing the crowd. The delighted audience cheered her and booed every attempt by Councillor Brookes to interrupt.

Then the mayor stood and beckoned to the two policemen. The little man fingered his chain and shrieked in a voice that silenced even Elizabeth Donovan. 'Eject that woman, constable. We will not have our business interrupted in this way. Throw her out!'

The audience, silenced, turned to watch the two constables, and as they turned to look, so did Elizabeth Donovan. She saw her daughter, dishevelled, untidy, dress torn, flourishing a roll of parchment.

'Peggy!' she called, in horror at the state of her daughter and, forgetting her mission to save the common, she clambered out of her seat. The people parted their ranks to let her through and watched as she rushed to her daughter in alarm.

166

'What on earth's happened to you, Peggy? Oh, Peggy!'

'Oh, Mum,' said Peggy, embarrassed at her mother's emotion.

'Oh, Mum, nothing,' said her mother. 'Look at you.' She seemed near to tears with concern. 'I'd better get you home, my love, and call a doctor.'

'But, Mum,' said Peggy. 'I've found it.'

'Found what?' asked Mrs Donovan.

The whole assembly watched in silence. Even the mayor and Councillor Brookes were silent. The chairman of the development company was shaking his head, as if to say this is no way to conduct important business. He got out his pen and moved to the dais to speak to Councillor Brookes.

It was Walter Lyons who recalled the meeting to its purpose.

'Gentlemen,' he called, and Councillor Brookes turned to look up at him. 'I wouldn't sign that agreement unless you want to face a long and costly legal battle that you're bound to lose.'

Brookes sneered. 'Take no notice,' he said clearly to the developer. 'A young man of very little sense.'

Walter smiled, walked down to the dais, and speaking as much to the audience as to Councillor Brookes, he said, 'I have here, due to the enterprise of the young lady up there,' he paused as everyone turned to look at Peggy, 'I have here a document that totally rules out the council's plans for the development on the common.'

'Pshaw!' said Councillor Brookes. 'Stuff and nonsense!'

'It is the deed of transfer between William Shelton Trafford, of Trafford Court, and the

Borough of Traverton, of the land known as Adam's Common. And it states, beyond any legal quibble, that Adam's Common may not, under any circumstances, be built on, that it must be maintained as a wild and natural place for the enjoyment of the children and people of Traverton in perpetuity.'

'That means forever,' came the piping voice of old Miss Trafford.

'Forever!' echoed two or three of the audience, and then the rest of them took up the cry, 'Forever! Adam's Common forever!'

'Adam's Common,' said Peggy as her mother bundled her into a taxi. 'Adam's Common,' she said again and sighed, forgetting the pain in her knee, her swollen ankle, and her bruises. 'Adam's Common forever.'

THIRTY-ONE

'Well,' said Mr Richards, 'there's a special item of news for you all.' He looked around the class and saw they were all in place.

'Come and sit at the front, Brookes. We can't have you lurking in the background.'

Tom Brookes grinned and ambled forward. He sat next to Peggy, nudged her with his elbow, winked, and grinned again.

Mr Richards surveyed the class again, and as he heard chatter coming from the rear of the class, his hand moved to his left ear. Before it got there, he dropped it.

He's in a very good mood, thought Peggy. He's beaming all over his face.

'Yes,' he began. 'You'll hear all this again tomorrow, in school assembly, but I thought I'd warn you first, so that you will be able to contain your enthusiasm.'

The class waited.

'The Trafford Award.' The class sighed. By now they had heard so much about the Trafford Award, and worked so hard toward it, that they would be glad to hear the end of it.

'Yes,' said Mr Richards. 'The award. It seems that it's Town School's year. I don't know the details but the headmaster has asked me to prepare you for the good news. So I think we can all guess the result. The headmaster said "good news". So that can only mean one thing. No,' he said quickly as he saw the class was about to break into cheers. 'Leave all that for tomorrow. But not too noisy tomorrow, either. As a very special tribute to the school, Miss Trafford is coming to make the presentations herself. She's an old lady, very old, well over ninety, and though – as you might say, Brookes – she's got all her marbles, she's frail and won't welcome the noise modern students make.'

He doesn't know her as well as I do, thought Peggy. I expect she'll enjoy it.

She was glad Town School was to be honoured by the Trafford Award. She had done nothing toward the survey but she knew how hard everyone else had worked and she was glad for them.

She found herself next to Marion Harper in assembly. She wanted to congratulate her, but there was not time.

The school stood in silence as the headmaster brought Miss Trafford, in her wheelchair, on to the platform.

'It's a proud day for us,' he began, 'and especially so because Miss Trafford has done us the honour of joining us. Today Miss Trafford is going to make the presentation of the Trafford Award. The award is given, I remind you, to the pupil or group of pupils, attending any school in the borough, who, in the eyes of the judges, have contributed most to the well-being of Traverton. I wish to say that this year, for the first time for many years, the decision of the judges was a unanimous one. I will now ask Miss Trafford to announce the winner of the Trafford Award and to present the medal.'

He wheeled Miss Trafford to the centre of the stage and whispered something.

'I know. I know,' she said, clearly and impatiently, her thin voice compelling attention.

'Headmaster,' she began. 'Staff and pupils of Town School. I know how . . .' She peered at a piece of paper in her hand. 'Oh, I can't be bothered with that,' she said and dropped it to the floor. 'The award goes to the girl who, by her courage and determination, saved Adam's Common for us all. Miss Peggy Donovan.'

There was a moment's silence and then a thunder of applause. Peggy felt Marion's hand clutching her arm, urging her to make her way forward. Peggy closed her eyes and opened them again. She could not believe it, and now she could not see, for her eyes were misting over. She made her way by instinct to the centre aisle and then walked to the platform and up the steps to Miss Trafford. No walk had ever seemed so long. She thought she might stumble and fall. She wished she had put on her regulation brown brogues. Someone would be bound to notice her casual shoes.

If they did, no one mentioned them. Every face on the platform was glowing with pleasure, and there was a specially proud look on Mr Richards's face.

'My dear,' said Miss Trafford, as Peggy bent down, 'you deserve it.' Peggy felt the wizened lips kiss her, and then she stood to face the school.

'Hold it up and show them,' said Miss Trafford in a stage whisper. 'It's years since Town School won it.'

She held the medal up to show it to the school. She saw it was engraved with the arms of the

Trafford family. She wondered if they would let her keep it, to take back home to Boston.

Home? But home was here, in Traverton, and she had left her own mark on it. It was home to her now, as it had been to William Shelton Trafford – and as it had once been to Adam.

Yes, she was at home, she decided, as she looked at her friends in the hall below.

THE END

MANY HAPPY RETURNS AND OTHER STORIES
by Kathryn Cave

Alice loathes all her birthday presents on sight and finds a hilarious way of dealing with them . . .

Cousin Roderick comes to stay and causes chaos until a spider provides an unusual solution . . .

The dreaded Mrs Bannerman terrorizes her class when mystery messages from 'Billy Molloy' appear on the blackboard. Who wrote them?

And just what *are* James and Mary going to do about the dinosaur in their garden?

These are just a few of the extremely funny and perceptive stories in this new collection from Kathryn Cave, author of the highly popular *Dragonrise*.

0 552 524344

CORGI

UNDERDOG
by Marilyn Sachs

No-one really seems to want Izzy when her
father dies. Packed off to live with her uncle and
aunt, she tries to rebuild her life in a very different family and in a strange new city.

Then Izzy finds a faded photograph of herself as
a child – and of Gus, the little dog she had once
loved. What has happened to Gus, and how is he
linked with her mother's mysterious death?

Izzy's desperate search for her dog leads her on
a journey into the past. But time is running out
for Gus . . .

0 552 524689

CORGI

GO TELL IT TO MRS GOLIGHTLY
by Catherine Cookson

'You've got to forget about Mrs Golightly!' So says Bella's cold, crusty grandfather when nine-year-old Bella Dodd, who is blind, is sent to stay with him after her father's death. Surely Mrs Golightly – who Bella talks of constantly – is just another of her imaginary friends, like Gip her dog?

But Bella is blind – not stupid. As Mrs Golightly would say, she had eyes in her brain and that was better than having them stuck in front of your face because people who had them there never saw anything. And it is Bella's quick wits and courage that are needed when she and her new-found friend, John, stumble across a dangerous plot that threatens all their lives, and that of a mysterious stranger . . .

An action-packed tale full of the strong, un-stoppable characters for which Catherine Cookson is famous.

0 552 52527 8

If you would like to receive a Newsletter about our new Children's books, just fill in the coupon below with your name and address (or copy it onto a separate piece of paper if you don't want to spoil your book) and send it to:

The Children's Books Editor
Young Corgi Books
61–63 Uxbridge Road,
Ealing
London W5 5SA

Please send me a Children's Newsletter:

Name . . . .

Address . . . .

. . . .

. . . .

All Children's Books are available at your bookshop or newsagent, or can be ordered from the following address:
Corgi/Bantam Books,
Cash Sales Department,
P.O. Box 11, Falmouth, Cornwall TR10 9EN

Please send a cheque or postal order (no currency) and allow 60p for postage and packing for the first book plus 25p for the second book and 15p for each additional book ordered up to a maximum charge of £1.90 in UK.

B.F.P.O. customers please allow 60p for the first book, 25p for the second book plus 15p per copy for the next 7 books, thereafter 9p per book.

Overseas customers, including Eire, please allow £1.25 for postage and packing for the first book, 75p for the second book, and 28p for each subsequent title ordered.